Samuel Langhorne Clemens (November 30, 1835 – April 21, 1910), known by his pen name Mark Twain, was an American writer, humorist, entrepreneur, publisher, and lecturer. He was lauded as the "greatest humorist this country has produced", and William Faulkner called him "the father of American literature". His novels include The Adventures of Tom Sawyer (1876) and its sequel, the Adventures of Huckleberry Finn (1884), the latter often called "The Great American Novel".

Twain was raised in Hannibal, Missouri, which later provided the setting for Tom Sawyer and Huckleberry Finn. He served an apprenticeship with a printer and then worked as a typesetter, contributing articles to the newspaper of his older brother Orion Clemens. He later became a riverboat pilot on the Mississippi River before heading west to join Orion in Nevada. (Source: Wikipedia)

Literary works:
The Gilded Age: A Tale of Today (1873)
The Prince and the Pauper (1881)
A Connecticut Yankee in
King Arthur's Court (1889)
The American Claimant (1892)
Pudd'nhead Wilson (1894)
Personal Recollections of Joan of Arc (1896)
A Horse's Tale (1907)
The Mysterious Stranger (1916, posthumous)
The Adventures of Tom Sawyer (1876)
Adventures of Huckleberry Finn (1884)
Tom Sawyer Abroad (1894)
Tom Sawyer, Detective (1896)
"Eve's Diary"(1906)

THOSE EXTRAORDINARY TWINS
MARK TWAIN

PRINCE CLASSICS

PRINCE CLASSICS

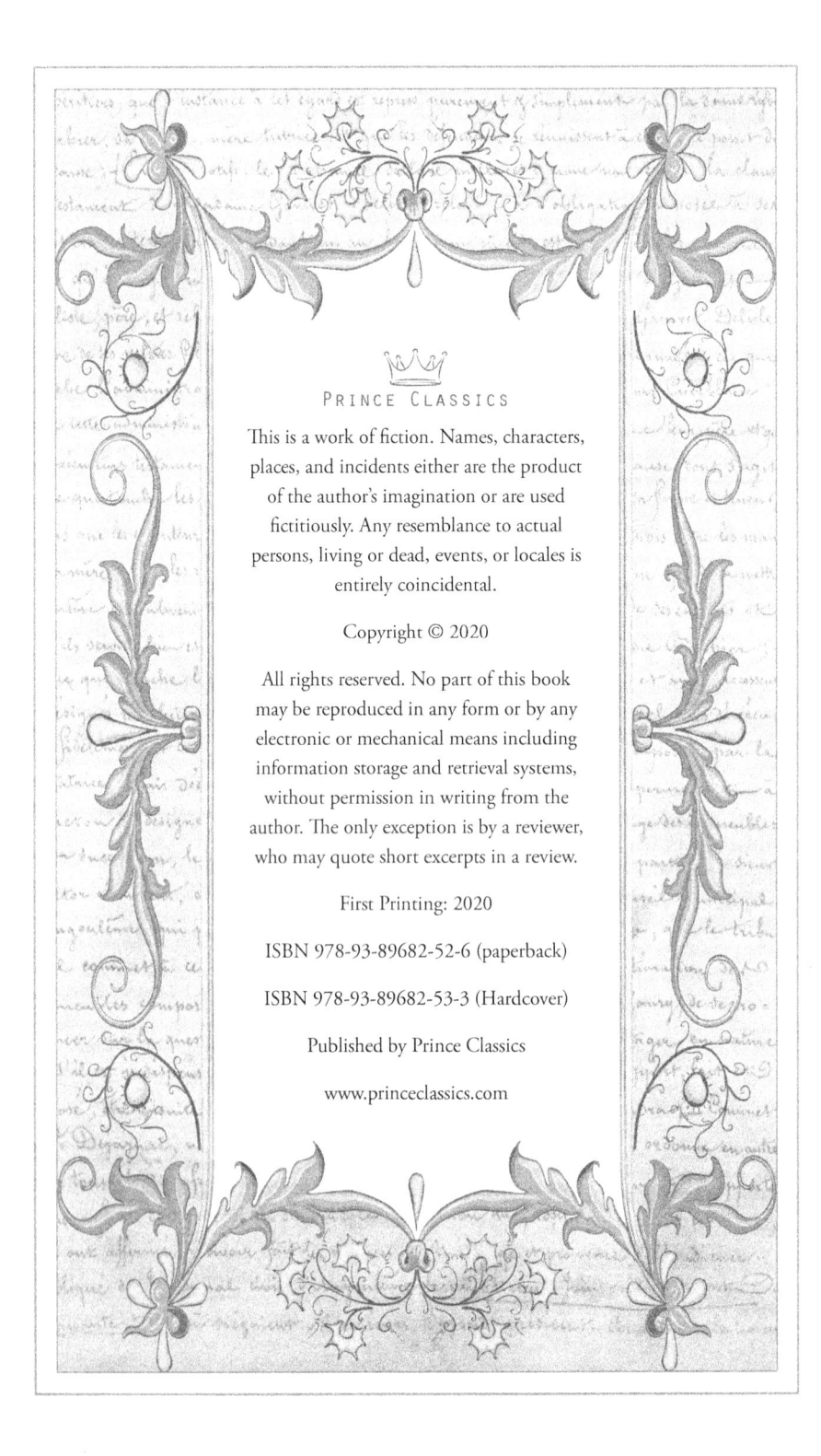

This is a work of fiction. Names, characters, places, and incidents either are the product of the author's imagination or are used fictitiously. Any resemblance to actual persons, living or dead, events, or locales is entirely coincidental.

Copyright © 2020

All rights reserved. No part of this book may be reproduced in any form or by any electronic or mechanical means including information storage and retrieval systems, without permission in writing from the author. The only exception is by a reviewer, who may quote short excerpts in a review.

First Printing: 2020

ISBN 978-93-89682-52-6 (paperback)

ISBN 978-93-89682-53-3 (Hardcover)

Published by Prince Classics

www.princeclassics.com

Contents

CHAPTER I. THE TWINS AS THEY REALLY WERE — 13

CHAPTER II. MA COOPER GETS ALL MIXED UP — 21

CHAPTER III. ANGELO IS BLUE — 29

CHAPTER IV. SUPERNATURAL CHRONOMETRY — 32

CHAPTER V. GUILT AND INNOCENCE FINELY BLENT — 40

CHAPTER VI. THE AMAZING DUEL — 56

CHAPTER VII. LUIGI DEFIES GALEN — 62

CHAPTER VIII. BAPTISM OF THE BETTER HALF — 68

CHAPTER IX. THE DRINKLESS DRUNK — 71

CHAPTER X. SO THEY HANGED LUIGI — 73

FINAL REMARKS — 75

About Author — 77

THOSE EXTRAORDINARY TWINS

A man who is not born with the novel-writing gift has a troublesome time of it when he tries to build a novel. I know this from experience. He has no clear idea of his story; in fact he has no story. He merely has some people in his mind, and an incident or two, also a locality. He knows these people, he knows the selected locality, and he trusts that he can plunge those people into those incidents with interesting results. So he goes to work. To write a novel? No—that is a thought which comes later; in the beginning he is only proposing to tell a little tale; a very little tale; a six-page tale. But as it is a tale which he is not acquainted with, and can only find out what it is by listening as it goes along telling itself, it is more than apt to go on and on and on till it spreads itself into a book. I know about this, because it has happened to me so many times.

And I have noticed another thing: that as the short tale grows into a long tale, the original intention (or motif) is apt to get abolished and find itself superseded by a quite different one. It was so in the case of a magazine sketch which I once started to write—a funny and fantastic sketch about a prince and a pauper; it presently assumed a grave cast of its own accord, and in that new shape spread itself out into a book. Much the same thing happened with "Pudd'nhead Wilson." I had a sufficiently hard time with that tale, because it changed itself from a farce to a tragedy while I was going along with it—a most embarrassing circumstance. But what was a great deal worse was, that it was not one story, but two stories tangled together; and they obstructed and interrupted each other at every turn and created no end of confusion and annoyance. I could not offer the book for publication, for I was afraid it would unseat the reader's reason. I did not know what was the matter with it, for I had not noticed, as yet, that it was two stories in one. It took me months to make that discovery. I carried the manuscript back and forth across the Atlantic two or three times, and read it and studied over it on shipboard; and at last I saw where the difficulty lay. I had no further trouble. I pulled one of the stories out by the roots, and left the other one—a kind of literary Caesarean operation.

Would the reader care to know something about the story which I pulled out? He has been told many a time how the born-and-trained novelist works. Won't he let me round and complete his knowledge by telling him how the jack-leg does it?

Originally the story was called "Those Extraordinary Twins." I meant to make it very short. I had seen a picture of a youthful Italian "freak" or "freaks" which was—or which were—on exhibition in our cities—a combination consisting of two heads and four arms joined to a single body and a single pair of legs—and I thought I would write an extravagantly fantastic little story with this freak of nature for hero—or heroes—a silly young miss for heroine, and two old ladies and two boys for the minor parts. I lavishly elaborated these people and their doings, of course. But the tale kept spreading along, and spreading along, and other people got to intruding themselves and taking up more and more room with their talk and their affairs. Among them came a stranger named Pudd'nhead Wilson, and a woman named Roxana; and presently the doings of these two pushed up into prominence a young fellow named Tom Driscoll, whose proper place was away in the obscure background. Before the book was half finished those three were taking things almost entirely into their own hands and working the whole tale as a private venture of their own—a tale which they had nothing at all to do with, by rights.

When the book was finished and I came to look around to see what had become of the team I had originally started out with—Aunt Patsy Cooper, Aunt Betsy Hale, the two boys, and Rowena the light-weight heroine—they were nowhere to be seen; they had disappeared from the story some time or other. I hunted about and found them—found them stranded, idle, forgotten, and permanently useless. It was very awkward. It was awkward all around; but more particularly in the case of Rowena, because there was a love-match on, between her and one of the twins that constituted the freak, and I had worked it up to a blistering heat and thrown in a quite dramatic love-quarrel, wherein Rowena scathingly denounced her betrothed for getting drunk, and scoffed at his explanation of how it had happened, and wouldn't listen to it, and had driven him from her in the usual "forever" way; and now here she sat crying and broken-hearted; for she had found that he had spoken only the truth; that it was not he, but the other half of the freak, that had drunk the liquor that made him drunk; that her half was a prohibitionist and had never drunk a drop in his life, and, although tight as a brick three days in the week, was wholly innocent of blame; and indeed, when sober, was constantly doing all he could to reform his brother, the other half, who never got any satisfaction out of drinking, anyway, because liquor never affected him. Yes, here she was, stranded with that deep injustice of hers torturing her poor torn heart.

I didn't know what to do with her. I was as sorry for her as anybody could be, but the campaign was over, the book was finished, she was sidetracked, and there was no possible way of crowding her in, anywhere. I could not leave her there, of course; it would not do. After spreading her out so, and making such a to-do over her affairs, it would be absolutely necessary to account to the reader for her. I thought and thought and studied and studied; but I arrived at nothing. I finally saw plainly that there was really no way but one—I must simply give her the grand bounce. It grieved me to do it, for after associating with her so much I had come to kind of like her after a fashion, notwithstanding she was such an ass and said such stupid irritating things and was so nauseatingly sentimental. Still it had to be done. So, at the top of Chapter XVII, I put in a "Calendar" remark concerning July the Fourth, and began the chapter with this statistic:

"Rowena went out in the back yard after supper to see the fireworks and fell down the well and got drowned."

It seemed abrupt, but I thought maybe the reader wouldn't notice it, because I changed the subject right away to something else. Anyway it loosened up Rowena from where she was stuck and got her out of the way, and that was the main thing. It seemed a prompt good way of weeding out people that had got stalled, and a plenty good enough way for those others; so I hunted up the two boys and said "they went out back one night to stone the cat and fell down the well and got drowned." Next I searched around and found old Aunt Patsy Cooper and Aunt Betsy Hale where they were aground, and said "they went out back one night to visit the sick and fell down the well and got drowned." I was going to drown some of the others, but I gave up the idea, partly because I believed that if I kept that up it would arouse attention, and perhaps sympathy with those people, and partly because it was not a large well and would not hold any more anyway.

Still the story was unsatisfactory. Here was a set of new characters who were become inordinately prominent and who persisted in remaining so to the end; and back yonder was an older set who made a large noise and a great to-do for a little while and then suddenly played out utterly and fell down the well. There was a radical defect somewhere, and I must search it out and cure it.

The defect turned out to be the one already spoken of—two stories in one, a farce and a tragedy. So I pulled out the farce and left the tragedy. This left the original team in, but only as mere names, not as characters. Their prominence was wholly gone; they were not even worth drowning; so I removed that detail. Also I took those twins apart and made two separate men of them. They had no occasion to have foreign names now, but it was too much trouble to remove them all through, so I left them christened as they were and made no explanation.

CHAPTER I. THE TWINS AS THEY REALLY WERE

The conglomerate twins were brought on the stage in Chapter I of the original extravaganza. Aunt Patsy Cooper has received their letter applying for board and lodging, and Rowena, her daughter, insane with joy, is begging for a hearing of it:

"Well, set down then, and be quiet a minute and don't fly around so; it fairly makes me tired to see you. It starts off so: 'HONORED MADAM'—"

"I like that, ma, don't you? It shows they're high-bred."

"Yes, I noticed that when I first read it. 'My brother and I have seen your advertisement, by chance, in a copy of your local journal—'"

"It's so beautiful and smooth, ma-don't you think so?"

"Yes, seems so to me—'and beg leave to take the room you offer. We are twenty-four years of age, and twins—'"

"Twins! How sweet! I do hope they are handsome, and I just know they are! Don't you hope they are, ma?"

"Land, I ain't particular. 'We are Italians by birth—'"

"It's so romantic! Just think there's never been one in this town, and everybody will want to see them, and they're all ours! Think of that!"

"—'but have lived long in the various countries of Europe, and several years in the United States.'"

"Oh, just think what wonders they've seen, ma! Won't it be good to hear them talk?"

"I reckon so; yes, I reckon so. 'Our names are Luigi and Angelo Capello—'"

"Beautiful, perfectly beautiful! Not like Jones and Robinson and those horrible names."

"'You desire but one guest, but dear madam, if you will allow us to pay for two we will not discommode you. We will sleep together in the same bed. We have always been used to this, and prefer it.' And then he goes on to say they will be down Thursday."

"And this is Tuesday—I don't know how I'm ever going to wait, ma! The time does drag along so, and I'm so dying to see them! Which of them do you reckon is the tallest, ma?"

"How do you s'pose I can tell, child? Mostly they are the same size-twins are."

"'Well then, which do you reckon is the best looking?"

"Goodness knows—I don't."

"I think Angelo is; it's the prettiest name, anyway. Don't you think it's a sweet name, ma?"

"Yes, it's well enough. I'd like both of them better if I knew the way to pronounce them—the Eyetalian way, I mean. The Missouri way and the Eyetalian way is different, I judge."

"Maybe—yes. It's Luigi that writes the letter. What do you reckon is the reason Angelo didn't write it?"

"Why, how can I tell? What's the difference who writes it, so long as it's done?"

"Oh, I hope it wasn't because he is sick! You don't think he is sick, do you, ma?"

"Sick your granny; what's to make him sick?"

"Oh, there's never any telling. These foreigners with that kind of names are so delicate, and of course that kind of names are not suited to our climate—you wouldn't expect it."

[And so-on and so-on, no end. The time drags along; Thursday comes: the boat arrives in a pouring storm toward midnight.]

At last there was a knock at the door and the anxious family jumped to open it. Two negro men entered, each carrying a trunk, and proceeded upstairs toward the guest-room. Then followed a stupefying apparition—a double-headed human creature with four arms, one body, and a single pair of legs! It—or they, as you please—bowed with elaborate foreign formality, but the Coopers could not respond immediately; they were paralyzed. At this moment there came from the rear of the group a fervent ejaculation—"My lan'!"—followed by a crash of crockery, and the slave-wench Nancy stood petrified and staring, with a tray of wrecked tea-things at her feet. The incident broke the spell, and brought the family to consciousness. The beautiful heads of the new-comer bowed again, and one of them said with easy grace and dignity:

"I crave the honor, madam and miss, to introduce to you my brother, Count Luigi Capello," (the other head bowed) "and myself—Count Angelo; and at the same time offer sincere apologies for the lateness of our coming, which was unavoidable," and both heads bowed again.

The poor old lady was in a whirl of amazement and confusion, but she managed to stammer out:

"I'm sure I'm glad to make your acquaintance, sir—I mean, gentlemen. As for the delay, it is nothing, don't mention it. This is my daughter Rowena, sir—gentlemen. Please step into the parlor and sit down and have a bite and sup; you are dreadful wet and must be uncomfortable—both of you, I mean."

But to the old lady's relief they courteously excused themselves, saying it would be wrong to keep the family out of their beds longer; then each head bowed in turn and uttered a friendly good night, and the singular figure moved away in the wake of Rowena's small brothers, who bore candles, and disappeared up the stairs.

The widow tottered into the parlor and sank into a chair with a gasp, and Rowena followed, tongue-tied and dazed. The two sat silent in the throbbing summer heat unconscious of the million-voiced music of the mosquitoes, unconscious of the roaring gale, the lashing and thrashing of the rain along the windows and the roof, the white glare of the lightning, the tumultuous booming and bellowing of the thunder; conscious of nothing but that prodigy, that uncanny apparition that had come and gone so suddenly—that weird strange thing that was so soft-spoken and so gentle of manner and yet had shaken them up like an earthquake with the shock of its gruesome aspect. At last a cold little shudder quivered along down the widow's meager frame and she said in a weak voice:

"Ugh, it was awful just the mere look of that phillipene!"

Rowena did not answer. Her faculties were still caked; she had not yet found her voice. Presently the widow said, a little resentfully:

"Always been used to sleeping together—in-fact, prefer it. And I was thinking it was to accommodate me. I thought it was very good of them, whereas a person situated as that young man is—"

"Ma, you oughtn't to begin by getting up a prejudice against him. I'm sure he is good-hearted and means well. Both of his faces show it."

"I'm not so certain about that. The one on the left—I mean the one on it's left—hasn't near as good a face, in my opinion, as its brother."

"That's Luigi."

"Yes, Luigi; anyway it's the dark-skinned one; the one that was west of his brother when they stood in the door. Up to all kinds of mischief and disobedience when he was a boy, I'll be bound. I lay his mother had trouble to lay her hand on him when she wanted him. But the one on the right is as good as gold, I can see that."

"That's Angelo."

"Yes, Angelo, I reckon, though I can't tell t'other from which by their names, yet awhile. But it's the right-hand one—the blond one. He has such kind blue eyes, and curly copper hair and fresh complexion—"

"And such a noble face!—oh, it is a noble face, ma, just royal, you may say! And beautiful deary me, how beautiful! But both are that; the dark one's as beautiful as—a picture. There's no such wonderful faces and handsome heads in this town none that even begin. And such hands, especially Angelo's—so shapely and—"

"Stuff, how could you tell which they belonged to?—they had gloves on."

"Why, didn't I see them take off their hats?"

"That don't signify. They might have taken off each other's hats. Nobody could tell. There was just a wormy squirming of arms in the air—seemed to be a couple of dozen of them, all writhing at once, and it just made me dizzy to see them go."

"Why, ma, I hadn't any difficulty. There's two arms on each shoulder—"

"There, now. One arm on each shoulder belongs to each of the creatures, don't it? For a person to have two arms on one shoulder wouldn't do him any good, would it? Of course not. Each has an arm on each shoulder. Now then, you tell me which of them belongs to which, if you can. They don't know, themselves—they just work whichever arm comes handy. Of course they do; especially if they are in a hurry and can't stop to think which belongs to which."

The mother seemed to have the rights of the argument, so the daughter abandoned the struggle. Presently the widow rose with a yawn and said:

"Poor thing, I hope it won't catch cold; it was powerful wet, just drenched, you may say. I hope it has left its boots outside, so they can be dried."

Then she gave a little start, and looked perplexed.

"Now I remember I heard one of them ask Joe to call him at half after seven—I think it was the one on the left—no, it was the one to the east of the other one—but I didn't hear the other one say any thing. I wonder if he wants to be called too. Do you reckon it's too late to ask?"

"Why, ma, it's not necessary. Calling one is calling both. If one gets up, the other's got to."

17

"Sho, of course; I never thought of that. Well, come along, maybe we can get some sleep, but I don't know, I'm so shook up with what we've been through."

The stranger had made an impression on the boys, too. They had a word of talk as they were getting to bed. Henry, the gentle, the humane, said:

"I feel ever so sorry for it, don't you, Joe?"

But Joe was a boy of this world, active, enterprising, and had a theatrical side to him:

"Sorry? Why, how you talk! It can't stir a step without attracting attention. It's just grand!"

Henry said, reproachfully:

"Instead of pitying it, Joe, you talk as if—"

"Talk as if what? I know one thing mighty certain: if you can fix me so I can eat for two and only have to stub toes for one, I ain't going to fool away no such chance just for sentiment."

The twins were wet and tired, and they proceeded to undress without any preliminary remarks. The abundance of sleeve made the partnership coat hard to get off, for it was like skinning a tarantula; but it came at last, after much tugging and perspiring. The mutual vest followed. Then the brothers stood up before the glass, and each took off his own cravat and collar. The collars were of the standing kind, and came high up under the ears, like the sides of a wheelbarrow, as required by the fashion of the day. The cravats were as broad as a bankbill, with fringed ends which stood far out to right and left like the wings of a dragon-fly, and this also was strictly in accordance with the fashion of the time. Each cravat, as to color, was in perfect taste, so far as its owner's complexion was concerned—a delicate pink, in the case of the blond brother, a violent scarlet in the case of the brunette—but as a combination they broke all the laws of taste known to civilization. Nothing more fiendish and irreconcilable than those shrieking and blaspheming colors could have been contrived. The wet boots gave no end of trouble—to Luigi. When they were off at last, Angelo said, with bitterness:

"I wish you wouldn't wear such tight boots, they hurt my feet."

Luigi answered with indifference:

"My friend, when I am in command of our body, I choose my apparel according to my own convenience, as I have remarked more than several times already. When you are in command, I beg you will do as you please."

Angelo was hurt, and the tears came into his eyes. There was gentle reproach in his voice, but, not anger, when he replied:

"Luigi, I often consult your wishes, but you never consult mine. When I am in command I treat you as a guest; I try to make you feel at home; when you are in command you treat me as an intruder, you make me feel unwelcome. It embarrasses me cruelly in company, for I can see that people notice it and comment on it."

"Oh, damn the people," responded the brother languidly, and with the air of one who is tired of the subject.

A slight shudder shook the frame of Angelo, but he said nothing and the conversation ceased. Each buttoned his own share of the nightshirt in silence; then Luigi, with Paine's Age of Reason in his hand, sat down in one chair and put his feet in another and lit his pipe, while Angelo took his Whole Duty of Man, and both began to read. Angelo presently began to cough; his coughing increased and became mixed with gaspings for breath, and he was finally obliged to make an appeal to his brother's humanity:

"Luigi, if you would only smoke a little milder tobacco, I am sure I could learn not to mind it in time, but this is so strong, and the pipe is so rank that—"

"Angelo, I wouldn't be such a baby! I have learned to smoke in a week, and the trouble is already over with me; if you would try, you could learn too, and then you would stop spoiling my comfort with your everlasting complaints."

"Ah, brother, that is a strong word—everlasting—and isn't quite fair. I only complain when I suffocate; you know I don't complain when we are in the open air."

"Well, anyway, you could learn to smoke yourself."

"But my principles, Luigi, you forget my principles. You would not have me do a thing which I regard as a sin?"

"Oh, bosh!"

The conversation ceased again, for Angelo was sick and discouraged and strangling; but after some time he closed his book and asked Luigi to sing "From Greenland's Icy Mountains" with him, but he would not, and when he tried to sing by himself Luigi did his best to drown his plaintive tenor with a rude and rollicking song delivered in a thundering bass.

After the singing there was silence, and neither brother was happy. Before blowing the light out Luigi swallowed half a tumbler of whisky, and Angelo, whose sensitive organization could not endure intoxicants of any kind, took a pill to keep it from giving him the headache.

CHAPTER II. MA COOPER GETS ALL MIXED UP

The family sat in the breakfast-room waiting for the twins to come down. The widow was quiet, the daughter was alive with happy excitement. She said:

"Ah, they're a boon, ma, just a boon! Don't you think so?"

"Laws, I hope so, I don't know."

"Why, ma, yes you do. They're so fine and handsome, and high-bred and polite, so every way superior to our gawks here in this village; why, they'll make life different from what it was—so humdrum and commonplace, you know—oh, you may be sure they're full of accomplishments, and knowledge of the world, and all that, that will be an immense advantage to society here. Don't you think so, ma?"

"Mercy on me, how should I know, and I've hardly set eyes on them yet." After a pause she added, "They made considerable noise after they went up."

"Noise? Why, ma, they were singing! And it was beautiful, too."

"Oh, it was well enough, but too mixed-up, seemed to me."

"Now, ma, honor bright, did you ever hear 'Greenland's Icy Mountains' sung sweeter—now did you?"

"If it had been sung by itself, it would have been uncommon sweet, I don't deny it; but what they wanted to mix it up with 'Old Bob Ridley' for, I can't make out. Why, they don't go together, at all. They are not of the same nature. 'Bob Ridley' is a common rackety slam-bang secular song, one of the rippingest and rantingest and noisiest there is. I am no judge of music, and I don't claim it, but in my opinion nobody can make those two songs go together right."

"Why, ma, I thought—"

"It don't make any difference what you thought, it can't be done. They tried it, and to my mind it was a failure. I never heard such a crazy uproar; seemed to me, sometimes, the roof would come off; and as for the cats—well, I've lived a many a year, and seen cats aggravated in more ways than one, but I've never seen cats take on the way they took on last night."

"Well, I don't think that that goes for anything, ma, because it is the nature of cats that any sound that is unusual—"

"Unusual! You may well call it so. Now if they are going to sing duets every night, I do hope they will both sing the same tune at the same time, for in my opinion a duet that is made up of two different tunes is a mistake; especially when the tunes ain't any kin to one another, that way."

"But, ma, I think it must be a foreign custom; and it must be right too; and the best way, because they have had every opportunity to know what is right, and it don't stand to reason that with their education they would do anything but what the highest musical authorities have sanctioned. You can't help but admit that, ma."

The argument was formidably strong; the old lady could not find any way around it; so, after thinking it over awhile she gave in with a sigh of discontent, and admitted that the daughter's position was probably correct. Being vanquished, she had no mind to continue the topic at that disadvantage, and was about to seek a change when a change came of itself. A footstep was heard on the stairs, and she said:

"There-he's coming!"

"They, ma—you ought to say they—it's nearer right."

The new lodger, rather shoutingly dressed but looking superbly handsome, stepped with courtly carnage into the trim little breakfast-room and put out all his cordial arms at once, like one of those pocket-knives with a multiplicity of blades, and shook hands with the whole family simultaneously. He was so easy and pleasant and hearty that all embarrassment presently thawed away and disappeared, and a cheery feeling of friendliness and comradeship took its place. He—or preferably they—were asked to occupy the seat of honor at the foot of the table. They consented with thanks, and carved the beefsteak with one set of their hands while they distributed it at the same time with the other set.

"Will you have coffee, gentlemen, or tea?"

"Coffee for Luigi, if you please, madam, tea for me."

"Cream and sugar?"

"For me, yes, madam; Luigi takes his coffee, black. Our natures differ a good deal from each other, and our tastes also."

The first time the negro girl Nancy appeared in the door and saw the two heads turned in opposite directions and both talking at once, then saw the commingling arms feed potatoes into one mouth and coffee into the other at the same time, she had to pause and pull herself out of a faintness that came over her; but after that she held her grip and was able to wait on the table with fair courage.

Conversation fell naturally into the customary grooves. It was a little jerky, at first, because none of the family could get smoothly through a sentence without a wabble in it here and a break there, caused by some new surprise in the way of attitude or gesture on the part of the twins. The weather suffered the most. The weather was all finished up and disposed of, as a subject, before the simple Missourians had gotten sufficiently wonted to the spectacle of one body feeding two heads to feel composed and reconciled in the presence of so bizarre a miracle. And even after everybody's mind became tranquilized there was still one slight distraction left: the hand that picked up a biscuit carried it to the wrong head, as often as any other way, and the wrong mouth devoured it. This was a puzzling thing, and marred the talk a little. It bothered the widow to such a degree that she presently dropped out of the conversation without knowing it, and fell to watching and guessing and talking to herself:

"Now that hand is going to take that coffee to—no, it's gone to the other mouth; I can't understand it; and Now, here is the dark-complected hand with a potato in its fork, I'll see what goes with it—there, the light-complected head's got it, as sure as I live!"

Finally Rowena said:

"Ma, what is the matter with you? Are you dreaming about something?"

The old lady came to herself and blushed; then she explained with the first random thing that came into her mind: "I saw Mr. Angelo take up Mr. Luigi's coffee, and I thought maybe he—sha'n't I give you a cup, Mr. Angelo?"

"Oh no, madam, I am very much obliged, but I never drink coffee, much as I would like to. You did see me take up Luigi's cup, it is true, but if you noticed, I didn't carry it to my mouth, but to his."

"Y-es, I thought you did: Did you mean to?"

"How?"

The widow was a little embarrassed again. She said:

"I don't know but what I'm foolish, and you mustn't mind; but you see, he got the coffee I was expecting to see you drink, and you got a potato that I thought he was going to get. So I thought it might be a mistake all around, and everybody getting what wasn't intended for him."

Both twins laughed and Luigi said:

"Dear madam, there wasn't any mistake. We are always helping each other that way. It is a great economy for us both; it saves time and labor. We have a system of signs which nobody can notice or understand but ourselves. If I am using both my hands and want some coffee, I make the sign and Angelo furnishes it to me; and you saw that when he needed a potato I delivered it."

"How convenient!"

"Yes, and often of the extremest value. Take the Mississippi boats, for instance. They are always overcrowded. There is table-room for only half of the passengers, therefore they have to set a second table for the second half. The stewards rush both parties, they give them no time to eat a satisfying meal, both divisions leave the table hungry. It isn't so with us. Angelo books himself for the one table, I book myself for the other. Neither of us eats anything at the other's table, but just simply works—works. Thus, you see there are four hands to feed Angelo, and the same four to feed me. Each of us eats two meals."

The old lady was dazed with admiration, and kept saying, "It is perfectly wonderful, perfectly wonderful" and the boy Joe licked his chops enviously, but said nothing—at least aloud.

"Yes," continued Luigi, "our construction may have its disadvantages—in fact, HAS—but it also has its compensations of one sort and another. Take travel, for instance. Travel is enormously expensive, in all countries; we have been obliged to do a vast deal of it—come, Angelo, don't put any more sugar in your tea, I'm just over one indigestion and don't want another right away—been obliged to do a deal of it, as I was saying. Well, we always travel as one person, since we occupy but one seat; so we save half the fare."

"How romantic!" interjected Rowena, with effusion.

"Yes, my dear young lady, and how practical too, and economical. In Europe, beds in the hotels are not charged with the board, but separately—another saving, for we stood to our rights and paid for the one bed only. The landlords often insisted that as both of us occupied the bed we ought—"

"No, they didn't," said Angelo. "They did it only twice, and in both cases it was a double bed—a rare thing in Europe—and the double bed gave them some excuse. Be fair to the landlords; twice doesn't constitute 'often.'"

"Well, that depends—that depends. I knew a man who fell down a well twice. He said he didn't mind the first time, but he thought the second time was once too often. Have I misused that word, Mrs. Cooper?"

"To tell the truth, I was afraid you had, but it seems to look, now, like you hadn't." She stopped, and was evidently struggling with the difficult problem a moment, then she added in the tone of one who is convinced without being converted, "It seems so, but I can't somehow tell why."

Rowena thought Luigi's retort was wonderfully quick and bright, and she remarked to herself with satisfaction that there wasn't any young native of Dawson's Landing that could have risen to the occasion like that. Luigi detected the applause in her face, and expressed his pleasure and his thanks with his eyes; and so eloquently withal, that the girl was proud and pleased, and hung out the delicate sign of it on her cheeks. Luigi went on, with animation:

"Both of us get a bath for one ticket, theater seat for one ticket, pew-rent is on the same basis, but at peep-shows we pay double."

"We have much to be thankful for," said Angelo, impressively, with a reverent light in his eye and a reminiscent tone in his voice, "we have been greatly blessed. As a rule, what one of us has lacked, the other, by the bounty of Providence, has been able to supply. My brother is hardy, I am not; he is very masculine, assertive, aggressive; I am much less so. I am subject to illness, he is never ill. I cannot abide medicines, and cannot take them, but he has no prejudice against them, and—"

"Why, goodness gracious," interrupted the widow, "when you are sick, does he take the medicine for you?"

"Always, madam."

"Why, I never heard such a thing in my life! I think it's beautiful of you."

"Oh, madam, it's nothing, don't mention it, it's really nothing at all."

"But I say it's beautiful, and I stick to it!" cried the widow, with a speaking moisture in her eye.

"A well brother to take the medicine for his poor sick brother—I wish I had such a son," and she glanced reproachfully at her boys. "I declare I'll never rest till I've shook you by the hand," and she scrambled out of her chair in a fever of generous enthusiasm, and made for the twins, blind with her tears, and began to shake. The boy Joe corrected her: "You're shaking the wrong one, ma."

This flurried her, but she made a swift change and went on shaking.

"Got the wrong one again, ma," said the boy.

"Oh, shut up, can't you!" said the widow, embarrassed and irritated. "Give me all your hands, I want to shake them all; for I know you are both just as good as you can be."

It was a victorious thought, a master-stroke of diplomacy, though that never occurred to her and she cared nothing for diplomacy. She shook the four hands in turn cordially, and went back to her place in a state of high and fine exultation that made her look young and handsome.

"Indeed I owe everything to Luigi," said Angelo, affectionately. "But for him I could not have survived our boyhood days, when we were friendless and poor—ah, so poor! We lived from hand to mouth-lived on the coarse fare of unwilling charity, and for weeks and weeks together not a morsel of food passed my lips, for its character revolted me and I could not eat it. But for Luigi I should have died. He ate for us both."

"How noble!" sighed Rowena.

"Do you hear that?" said the widow, severely, to her boys. "Let it be an example to you—I mean you, Joe."

Joe gave his head a barely perceptible disparaging toss and said: "Et for both. It ain't anything I'd 'a' done it."

"Hush, if you haven't got any better manners than that. You don't see the point at all. It wasn't good food."

"I don't care—it was food, and I'd 'a' et it if it was rotten."

"Shame! Such language! Can't you understand? They were starving—actually starving—and he ate for both, and—"

"Shucks! you gimme a chance and I'll—"

"There, now—close your head! and don't you open it again till you're asked."

[*Angelo goes on and tells how his parents the Count and Countess had to fly from Florence for political reasons, and died poor in Berlin bereft of their great property by confiscation; and how he and Luigi had to travel with a freak-show during two years and suffer semi-starvation.]*

"That hateful black-bread; but I seldom ate anything during that time; that was poor Luigi's affair—"

"I'll never Mister him again!" cried the widow, with strong emotion, "he's Luigi to me, from this out!"

"Thank you a thousand times, madam, a thousand times! though in truth I don't deserve it."

"Ah, Luigi is always the fortunate one when honors are showering," said Angelo, plaintively; "now what have I done, Mrs. Cooper, that you leave me out? Come, you must strain a point in my favor."

"Call you Angelo? Why, certainly I will; what are you thinking of! In the case of twins, why—"

"But, ma, you're breaking up the story—do let him go on."

"You keep still, Rowena Cooper, and he can go on all the better, I reckon. One interruption don't hurt, it's two that makes the trouble."

"But you've added one, now, and that is three."

"Rowena! I will not allow you to talk back at me when you have got nothing rational to say."

CHAPTER III. ANGELO IS BLUE

[After breakfast the whole village crowded in, and there was a grand reception in honor of the twins; and at the close of it the gifted "freak" captured everybody's admiration by sitting down at the piano and knocking out a classic four-handed piece in great style. Then the judge took it—or them—driving in his buggy and showed off his village.]

All along the streets the people crowded the windows and stared at the amazing twins. Troops of small boys flocked after the buggy, excited and yelling. At first the dogs showed no interest. They thought they merely saw three men in a buggy—a matter of no consequence; but when they found out the facts of the case, they altered their opinion pretty radically, and joined the boys, expressing their minds as they came. Other dogs got interested; indeed, all the dogs. It was a spirited sight to see them come leaping fences, tearing around corners, swarming out of every bystreet and alley. The noise they made was something beyond belief—or praise. They did not seem to be moved by malice but only by prejudice, the common human prejudice against lack of conformity. If the twins turned their heads, they broke and fled in every direction, but stopped at a safe distance and faced about; and then formed and came on again as soon as the strangers showed them their back. Negroes and farmers' wives took to the woods when the buggy came upon them suddenly, and altogether the drive was pleasant and animated, and a refreshment all around.

> [It was a long and lively drive. Angelo was a Methodist, Luigi was a Free-thinker. The judge was very proud of his Freethinkers' Society, which was flourishing along in a most prosperous way and already had two members—himself and the obscure and neglected Pudd'nhead Wilson. It was to meet that evening, and he invited Luigi to join; a thing which Luigi was glad to do, partly because it

would please himself, and partly because it would gravel Angelo.]

They had now arrived at the widow's gate, and the excursion was ended. The twins politely expressed their obligations for the pleasant outing which had been afforded them; to which the judge bowed his thanks, and then said he would now go and arrange for the Free-thinkers' meeting, and would call for Count Luigi in the evening.

"For you also, dear sir," he added hastily, turning to Angelo and bowing. "In addressing myself particularly to your brother, I was not meaning to leave you out. It was an unintentional rudeness, I assure you, and due wholly to accident—accident and preoccupation. I beg you to forgive me."

His quick eye had seen the sensitive blood mount into Angelo's face, betraying the wound that had been inflicted. The sting of the slight had gone deep, but the apology was so prompt, and so evidently sincere, that the hurt was almost immediately healed, and a forgiving smile testified to the kindly judge that all was well again.

Concealed behind Angelo's modest and unassuming exterior, and unsuspected by any but his intimates, was a lofty pride, a pride of almost abnormal proportions, indeed, and this rendered him ever the prey of slights; and although they were almost always imaginary ones, they hurt none the less on that account. By ill fortune judge Driscoll had happened to touch his sorest point, i.e., his conviction that his brother's presence was welcomer everywhere than his own; that he was often invited, out of mere courtesy, where only his brother was wanted, and that in a majority of cases he would not be included in an invitation if he could be left out without offense. A sensitive nature like this is necessarily subject to moods; moods which traverse the whole gamut of feeling; moods which know all the climes of emotion, from the sunny heights of joy to the black abysses of despair. At times, in his seasons of deepest depressions, Angelo almost wished that he and his brother might become segregated from each other and be separate individuals, like other men. But of course as soon as his mind cleared and these diseased imaginings passed away, he shuddered at the repulsive thought, and earnestly prayed that it might visit him no more. To be separate, and as other men are! How awkward it would seem; how unendurable. What would he do with his hands, his arms? How would his legs feel? How odd, and strange, and grotesque every action, attitude, movement, gesture would be. To sleep by himself, eat by himself, walk by himself—how lonely, how unspeakably lonely! No, no, any fate but that. In every way and from every point, the idea was revolting.

This was of course natural; to have felt otherwise would have been unnatural. He had known no life but a combined one; he had been familiar with it from his birth; he was not able to conceive of any other as being agreeable, or even bearable. To him, in the privacy of his secret thoughts, all other men were monsters, deformities: and during three-fourths of his life their aspect had filled him with what promised to be an unconquerable aversion. But at eighteen his eye began to take note of female beauty; and little by little, undefined longings grew up in his heart, under whose softening influences the old stubborn aversion gradually diminished, and finally disappeared. Men were still monstrosities to him, still deformities, and in his sober moments he had no desire to be like them, but their strange and unsocial and uncanny construction was no longer offensive to him.

This had been a hard day for him, physically and mentally. He had been called in the morning before he had quite slept off the effects of the liquor which Luigi had drunk; and so, for the first half-hour had had the seedy feeling, and languor, the brooding depression, the cobwebby mouth and druggy taste that come of dissipation and are so ill a preparation for bodily or intellectual activities; the long violent strain of the reception had followed; and this had been followed, in turn, by the dreary sight-seeing, the judge's wearying explanations and laudations of the sights, and the stupefying clamor of the dogs. As a congruous conclusion, a fitting end, his feelings had been hurt, a slight had been put upon him. He would have been glad to forego dinner and betake himself to rest and sleep, but he held his peace and said no word, for he knew his brother, Luigi, was fresh, unweary, full of life, spirit, energy; he would have scoffed at the idea of wasting valuable time on a bed or a sofa, and would have refused permission.

CHAPTER IV. SUPERNATURAL CHRONOMETRY

Rowena was dining out, Joe and Harry were belated at play, there were but three chairs and four persons that noon at the home dinner-table—the twins, the widow, and her chum, Aunt Betsy Hale. The widow soon perceived that Angelo's spirits were as low as Luigi's were high, and also that he had a jaded look. Her motherly solicitude was aroused, and she tried to get him interested in the talk and win him to a happier frame of mind, but the cloud of sadness remained on his countenance. Luigi lent his help, too. He used a form and a phrase which he was always accustomed to employ in these circumstances. He gave his brother an affectionate slap on the shoulder and said, encouragingly:

"Cheer up, the worst is yet to come!"

But this did no good. It never did. If anything, it made the matter worse, as a rule, because it irritated Angelo. This made it a favorite with Luigi. By and by the widow said:

"Angelo, you are tired, you've overdone yourself; you go right to bed after dinner, and get a good nap and a rest, then you'll be all right."

"Indeed, I would give anything if I could do that, madam."

"And what's to hender, I'd like to know? Land, the room's yours to do what you please with! The idea that you can't do what you like with your own!"

"But, you see, there's one prime essential—an essential of the very first importance—which isn't my own."

"What is that?"

"My body."

The old ladies looked puzzled, and Aunt Betsy Hale said:

"Why bless your heart, how is that?"

"It's my brother's."

"Your brother's! I don't quite understand. I supposed it belonged to both of you."

"So it does. But not to both at the same time."

"That is mighty curious; I don't see how it can be. I shouldn't think it could be managed that way."

"Oh, it's a good enough arrangement, and goes very well; in fact, it wouldn't do to have it otherwise. I find that the teetotalers and the anti-teetotalers hire the use of the same hall for their meetings. Both parties don't use it at the same time, do they?"

"You bet they don't!" said both old ladies in a breath.

"And, moreover," said Aunt Betsy, "the Freethinkers and the Baptist Bible class use the same room over the Market house, but you can take my word for it they don't mush up together and use it at the same time.'

"Very well," said Angelo, "you understand it now. And it stands to reason that the arrangement couldn't be improved. I'll prove it to you. If our legs tried to obey two wills, how could we ever get anywhere? I would start one way, Luigi would start another, at the same moment—the result would be a standstill, wouldn't it?"

"As sure as you are born! Now ain't that wonderful! A body would never have thought of it."

"We should always be arguing and fussing and disputing over the merest trifles. We should lose worlds of time, for we couldn't go down-stairs or up, couldn't go to bed, couldn't rise, couldn't wash, couldn't dress, couldn't stand up, couldn't sit down, couldn't even cross our legs, without calling a meeting first and explaining the case and passing resolutions, and getting consent. It wouldn't ever do—now would it?"

"Do? Why, it would wear a person out in a week! Did you ever hear anything like it, Patsy Cooper?"

"Oh, you'll find there's more than one thing about them that ain't commonplace," said the widow, with the complacent air of a person with a property right in a novelty that is under admiring scrutiny.

"Well, now, how ever do you manage it? I don't mind saying I'm suffering to know."

"He who made us," said Angelo reverently, "and with us this difficulty, also provided a way out of it. By a mysterious law of our being, each of us has utter and indisputable command of our body a week at a time, turn and turn about."

"Well, I never! Now ain't that beautiful!"

"Yes, it is beautiful and infinitely wise and just. The week ends every Saturday at midnight to the minute, to the second, to the last shade of a fraction of a second, infallibly, unerringly, and in that instant the one brother's power over the body vanishes and the other brother takes possession, asleep or awake."

"How marvelous are His ways, and past finding out!"

Luigi said: "So exactly to the instant does the change come, that during our stay in many of the great cities of the world, the public clocks were regulated by it; and as hundreds of thousands of private clocks and watches were set and corrected in accordance with the public clocks, we really furnished the standard time for the entire city."

"Don't tell me that He don't do miracles any more! Blowing down the walls of Jericho with rams' horns wa'n't as difficult, in my opinion."

"And that is not all," said Angelo. "A thing that is even more marvelous, perhaps, is the fact that the change takes note of longitude and fits itself to the meridian we are on. Luigi is in command this week. Now, if on Saturday night at a moment before midnight we could fly in an instant to a point fifteen degrees west of here, he would hold possession of the power another hour, for the change observes local time and no other."

Betsy Hale was deeply impressed, and said with solemnity:

"Patsy Cooper, for detail it lays over the Passage of the Red Sea."

"Now, I shouldn't go as far as that," said Aunt Patsy, "but if you've a mind to say Sodom and Gomorrah, I am with you, Betsy Hale."

"I am agreeable, then, though I do think I was right, and I believe Parson Maltby would say the same. Well, now, there's another thing. Suppose one of you wants to borrow the legs a minute from the one that's got them, could he let him?"

"Yes, but we hardly ever do that. There were disagreeable results, several times, and so we very seldom ask or grant the privilege, nowadays, and we never even think of such a thing unless the case is extremely urgent. Besides, a week's possession at a time seems so little that we can't bear to spare a minute of it. People who have the use of their legs all the time never think of what a blessing it is, of course. It never occurs to them; it's just their natural ordinary condition, and so it does not excite them at all. But when I wake up, on Sunday morning, and it's my week and I feel the power all through me, oh, such a wave of exultation and thanksgiving goes surging over me, and I want to shout 'I can walk! I can walk!' Madam, do you ever, at your uprising, want to shout 'I can walk! I can walk!'?"

"No, you poor unfortunate cretur', but I'll never get out of my bed again without doing it! Laws, to think I've had this unspeakable blessing all my long life and never had the grace to thank the good Lord that gave it to me!"

Tears stood in the eyes of both the old ladies and the widow said, softly:

"Betsy Hale, we have learned something, you and me."

The conversation now drifted wide, but by and by floated back once more to that admired detail, the rigid and beautiful impartiality with which the possession of power had been distributed, between the twins. Aunt Betsy saw in it a far finer justice than human law exhibits in related cases. She said:

"In my opinion it ain't right noW, and never has been right, the way a twin born a quarter of a minute sooner than the other one gets all the land

and grandeurs and nobilities in the old countries and his brother has to go bare and be a nobody. Which of you was born first?"

Angelo's head was resting against Luigi's; weariness had overcome him, and for the past five minutes he had been peacefully sleeping. The old ladies had dropped their voices to a lulling drone, to help him to steal the rest his brother wouldn't take him up-stairs to get. Luigi listened a moment to Angelo's regular breathing, then said in a voice barely audible:

"We were both born at the same time, but I am six months older than he is."

"For the land's sake!"

"'Sh! don't wake him up; he wouldn't like my telling this. It has always been kept secret till now."

"But how in the world can it be? If you were both born at the same time, how can one of you be older than the other?"

"It is very simple, and I assure you it is true. I was born with a full crop of hair, he was as bald as an egg for six months. I could walk six months before he could make a step. I finished teething six months ahead of him. I began to take solids six months before he left the breast. I began to talk six months before he could say a word. Last, and absolutely unassailable proof, the sutures in my skull closed six months ahead of his. Always just that six months' difference to a day. Was that accident? Nobody is going to claim that, I'm sure. It was ordained—it was law—it had its meaning, and we know what that meaning was. Now what does this overwhelming body of evidence establish? It establishes just one thing, and that thing it establishes beyond any peradventure whatever. Friends, we would not have it known for the world, and I must beg you to keep it strictly to yourselves, but the truth is, we are no more twins than you are."

The two old ladies were stunned, paralyzed—petrified, one may almost say—and could only sit and gaze vacantly at each other for some moments; then Aunt Betsy Hale said impressively:

"There's no getting around proof like that. I do believe it's the most amazing thing I ever heard of." She sat silent a moment or two and breathing hard with excitement, then she looked up and surveyed the strangers steadfastly a little while, and added: "Well, it does beat me, but I would have took you for twins anywhere."

"So would I, so would I," said Aunt Patsy with the emphasis of a certainty that is not impaired by any shade of doubt.

"Anybody would-anybody in the world, I don't care who he is," said Aunt Betsy with decision.

"You won't tell," said Luigi, appealingly.

"Oh, dear, no!" answered both ladies promptly, "you can trust us, don't you be afraid."

"That is good of you, and kind. Never let on; treat us always as if we were twins."

"You can depend on us," said Aunt Betsy, "but it won't be easy, because now that I know you ain't you don't seem so."

Luigi muttered to himself with satisfaction: "That swindle has gone through without change of cars."

It was not very kind of him to load the poor things up with a secret like that, which would be always flying to their tongues' ends every time they heard any one speak of the strangers as twins, and would become harder and harder to hang on to with every recurrence of the temptation to tell it, while the torture of retaining it would increase with every new strain that was applied; but he never thought of that, and probably would not have worried much about it if he had.

A visitor was announced—some one to see the twins. They withdrew to the parlor, and the two old ladies began to discuss with interest the strange things which they had been listening to. When they had finished the matter to their satisfaction, and Aunt Betsy rose to go, she stopped to ask a question:

"How does things come on between Roweny and Tom Driscoll?"

"Well, about the same. He writes tolerable often, and she answers tolerable seldom."

"Where is he?"

"In St. Louis, I believe, though he's such a gadabout that a body can't be very certain of him, I reckon."

"Don't Roweny know?"

"Oh, yes, like enough. I haven't asked her lately."

"Do you know how him and the judge are getting along now?"

"First rate, I believe. Mrs. Pratt says so; and being right in the house, and sister to the one and aunt to t'other, of course she ought to know. She says the judge is real fond of him when he's away; but frets when he's around and is vexed with his ways, and not sorry to have him go again. He has been gone three weeks this time—a pleasant thing for both of them, I reckon."

"Tom's rather harum-scarum, but there ain't anything bad in him, I guess."

"Oh, no, he's just young, that's all. Still, twenty-three is old, in one way. A young man ought to be earning his living by that time. If Tom were doing that, or was even trying to do it, the judge would be a heap better satisfied with him. Tom's always going to begin, but somehow he can't seem to find just the opening he likes."

"Well, now, it's partly the judge's own fault. Promising the boy his property wasn't the way to set him to earning a fortune of his own. But what do you think—is Roweny beginning to lean any toward him, or ain't she?"

Aunt Patsy had a secret in her bosom; she wanted to keep it there, but nature was too strong for her. She drew Aunt Betsy aside, and said in her most confidential and mysterious manner:

"Don't you breathe a syllable to a soul—I'm going to tell you something.

In my opinion Tom Driscoll's chances were considerable better yesterday than they are to-day."

"Patsy Cooper, what do you mean?"

"It's so, as sure as you're born. I wish you could 'a' been at breakfast and seen for yourself."

"You don't mean it!"

"Well, if I'm any judge, there's a leaning—there's a leaning, sure."

"My land! Which one of 'em is it?"

"I can't say for certain, but I think it's the youngest one—Anjy."

Then there were hand-shakings, and congratulations, and hopes, and so on, and the old ladies parted, perfectly happy—the one in knowing something which the rest of the town didn't, and the other in having been the sole person able to furnish that knowledge.

The visitor who had called to see the twins was the Rev. Mr. Hotchkiss, pastor of the Baptist church. At the reception Angelo had told him he had lately experienced a change in his religious views, and was now desirous of becoming a Baptist, and would immediately join Mr. Hotchkiss's church. There was no time to say more, and the brief talk ended at that point. The minister was much gratified, and had dropped in for a moment now, to invite the twins to attend his Bible class at eight that evening. Angelo accepted, and was expecting Luigi to decline, but he did not, because he knew that the Bible class and the Freethinkers met in the same room, and he wanted to treat his brother to the embarrassment of being caught in free-thinking company.

CHAPTER V. GUILT AND INNOCENCE FINELY BLENT

[A long and vigorous quarrel follows, between the twins. And there is plenty to quarrel about, for Angelo was always seeking truth, and this obliged him to change and improve his religion with frequency, which wearied Luigi, and annoyed him too; for he had to be present at each new enlistment—which placed him in the false position of seeming to indorse and approve his brother's fickleness; moreover, he had to go to Angelo's prohibition meetings, and he hated them. On the other hand, when it was his week to command the legs he gave Angelo just cause of complaint, for he took him to circuses and horse-races and fandangoes, exposing him to all sorts of censure and criticism; and he drank, too; and whatever he drank went to Angelo's head instead of his own and made him act disgracefully. When the evening was come, the two attended the Free-thinkers' meeting, where Angelo was sad and silent; then came the Bible class and looked upon him coldly, finding him in such company. Then they went to Wilson's house and Chapter XI of Pudd'nhead Wilson follows, which tells of the girl seen in Tom Driscoll's room; and closes with the kicking of Tom by Luigi at the anti-temperance mass-meeting of the Sons of Liberty; with the addition of some account of Roxy's adventures as a chamber-maid on a Mississippi boat. Her exchange of the children had been flippantly and farcically described in an earlier chapter.]

Next morning all the town was a-buzz with great news; Pudd'nhead Wilson had a law case! The public astonishment was so great and the public curiosity so intense, that when the justice of the peace opened his court, the place was packed with people and even the windows were full. Everybody was flushed and perspiring; the summer heat was almost unendurable.

Tom Driscoll had brought a charge of assault and battery against the twins. Robert Allen was retained by Driscoll, David Wilson by the defense. Tom, his native cheerfulness unannihilated by his back-breaking and bone-bruising passage across the massed heads of the Sons of Liberty the previous night, laughed his little customary laugh, and said to Wilson:

"I've kept my promise, you see; I'm throwing my business your way. Sooner than I was expecting, too."

"It's very good of you—particularly if you mean to keep it up."

"Well, I can't tell about that yet. But we'll see. If I find you deserve it I'll take you under my protection and make your fame and fortune for you."

"I'll try to deserve it, Tom."

A jury was sworn in; then Mr. Allen said:

"We will detain your honor but a moment with this case. It is not one where any doubt of the fact of the assault can enter in. These gentlemen—the accused—kicked my client at the Market Hall last night; they kicked him with violence; with extraordinary violence; with even unprecedented violence, I may say; insomuch that he was lifted entirely off his feet and discharged into the midst of the audience. We can prove this by four hundred witnesses—we shall call but three. Mr. Harkness will take the stand."

Mr. Harkness, being sworn, testified that he was chairman upon the occasion mentioned; that he was close at hand and saw the defendants in this action kick the plaintiff into the air and saw him descend among the audience.

"Take the witness," said Allen.

"Mr. Harkness," said Wilson, "you say you saw these gentlemen, my clients, kick the plaintiff. Are you sure—and please remember that you are on oath—are you perfectly sure that you saw both of them kick him, or only one? Now be careful."

A bewildered look began to spread itself over the witness's face. He hesitated, stammered, but got out nothing. His eyes wandered to the twins and fixed themselves there with a vacant gaze.

"Please answer, Mr. Harkness, you are keeping the court waiting. It is a very simple question."

Counsel for the prosecution broke in with impatience:

"Your honor, the question is an irrelevant triviality. Necessarily, they both kicked him, for they have but the one pair of legs, and both are responsible for them."

Wilson said, sarcastically:

"Will your honor permit this new witness to be sworn? He seems to possess knowledge which can be of the utmost value just at this moment—knowledge which would at once dispose of what every one must see is a very difficult question in this case. Brother Allen, will you take the stand?"

"Go on with your case!" said Allen, petulantly. The audience laughed, and got a warning from the court.

"Now, Mr. Harkness," said Wilson, insinuatingly, "we shall have to insist upon an answer to that question."

"I—er—well, of course, I do not absolutely know, but in my opinion—"

"Never mind your opinion, sir—answer the question."

"I—why, I can't answer it."

"That will do, Mr. Harkness. Stand down."

The audience tittered, and the discomfited witness retired in a state of great embarrassment.

Mr. Wakeman took the stand and swore that he saw the twins kick the plaintiff off the platform.

The defense took the witness.

"Mr. Wakeman, you have sworn that you saw these gentlemen kick the plaintiff. Do I understand you to swear that you saw them both do it?"

"Yes, sir,"—with decision.

"How do you know that both did it?"

"Because I saw them do it."

The audience laughed, and got another warning from the court.

"But by what means do you know that both, and not one, did it?"

"Well, in the first place, the insult was given to both of them equally, for they were called a pair of scissors. Of course they would both want to resent it, and so—"

"Wait! You are theorizing now. Stick to facts—counsel will attend to the arguments. Go on."

"Well, they both went over there—that I saw."

"Very good. Go on."

"And they both kicked him—I swear to it."

"Mr. Wakeman, was Count Luigi, here, willing to join the Sons of Liberty last night?"

"Yes, sir, he was. He did join, too, and drank a glass or two of whisky, like a man."

"Was his brother willing to join?"

"No, sir, he wasn't. He is a teetotaler, and was elected through a mistake."

"Was he given a glass of whisky?"

"Yes, sir, but of course that was another mistake, and not intentional. He wouldn't drink it. He set it down." A slight pause, then he added, casually and quite simply: "The plaintiff reached for it and hogged it."

There was a fine outburst of laughter, but as the justice was caught out himself, his reprimand was not very vigorous.

Mr. Allen jumped up and exclaimed: "I protest against these foolish irrelevancies. What have they to do with the case?"

Wilson said: "Calm yourself, brother, it was only an experiment. Now, Mr. Wakeman, if one of these gentlemen chooses to join an association and the other doesn't; and if one of them enjoys whisky and the other doesn't, but sets it aside and leaves it unprotected" (titter from the audience), "it seems to show that they have independent minds, and tastes, and preferences, and that one of them is able to approve of a thing at the very moment that the other is heartily disapproving of it. Doesn't it seem so to you?"

"Certainly it does. It's perfectly plain."

"Now, then, it might be—I only say it might be—that one of these brothers wanted to kick the plaintiff last night, and that the other didn't want that humiliating punishment inflicted upon him in that public way and before all those people. Isn't that possible?"

"Of course it is. It's more than possible. I don't believe the blond one would kick anybody. It was the other one that—"

"Silence!" shouted the plaintiff's counsel, and went on with an angry sentence which was lost in the wave of laughter that swept the house.

"That will do, Mr. Wakeman," said Wilson, "you may stand down."

The third witness was called. He had seen the twins kick the plaintiff. Mr. Wilson took the witness.

"Mr. Rogers, you say you saw these accused gentlemen kick the plaintiff?"

"Yes, sir."

"Both of them?"

"Yes, sir."

"Which of them kicked him first?"

"Why—they—they both kicked him at the same time.

"Are you perfectly sure of that?"

"Yes, sir."

"What makes you sure of it?"

"Why, I stood right behind them, and saw them do it."

"How many kicks were delivered?"

"Only one."

"If two men kick, the result should be two kicks, shouldn't it?"

"Why—why yes, as a rule."

"Then what do you think went with the other kick?"

"I—well—the fact is, I wasn't thinking of two being necessary, this time."

"What do you think now?"

"Well, I—I'm sure I don't quite know what to think, but I reckon that one of them did half of the kick and the other one did the other half."

Somebody in the crowd sung out: "It's the first sane thing that any of them has said."

The audience applauded. The judge said: "Silence! or I will clear the court."

Mr. Allen looked pleased, but Wilson did not seem disturbed. He said:

"Mr. Rogers, you have favored us with what you think and what you reckon, but as thinking and reckoning are not evidence, I will now give you a chance to come out with something positive, one way or the other, and shall require you to produce it. I will ask the accused to stand up and repeat the phenomenal kick of last night." The twins stood up. "Now, Mr. Rogers, please stand behind them."

A Voice: "No, stand in front!" (Laughter. Silenced by the court.) Another Voice: "No, give Tommy another highst!" (Laughter. Sharply rebuked by the court.)

"Now, then, Mr. Rogers, two kicks shall be delivered, one after the other, and I give you my word that at least one of the two shall be delivered by one of the twins alone, without the slightest assistance from his brother. Watch sharply, for you have got to render a decision without any if's and ands it." Rogers bent himself behind the twins with his palms just above his knees, in the modern attitude of the catcher at a baseball match, and riveted his eyes on the pair of legs in front of him.

"Are you ready, Mr. Rogers?"

"Ready sir."

The kick was launched.

"Have you got that one classified, Mr. Rogers?"

"Let me study a minute, sir."

"Take as much time as you please. Let me know when you are ready."

For as much as a minute Rogers pondered, with all eyes and a breathless interest fastened upon him. Then he gave the word: "Ready, sir."

"Kick!"

The kick that followed was an exact duplicate of the first one.

"Now, then, Mr. Rogers, one of those kicks was an individual kick, not a mutual one. You will now state positively which was the mutual one."

The witness said, with a crestfallen look:

"I've got to give it up. There ain't any man in the world that could tell t'other from which, sir."

"Do you still assert that last night's kick was a mutual kick?"

"Indeed, I don't, sir."

"That will do, Mr. Rogers. If my brother Allen desires to address the court, your honor, very well; but as far as I am concerned I am ready to let the case be at once delivered into the hands of this intelligent jury without comment."

Mr. Justice Robinson had been in office only two months, and in that short time had not had many cases to try, of course. He had no knowledge of laws and courts except what he had picked up since he came into office. He was a sore trouble to the lawyers, for his rulings were pretty eccentric sometimes, and he stood by them with Roman simplicity and fortitude; but the people were well satisfied with him, for they saw that his intentions were always right, that he was entirely impartial, and that he usually made up in good sense what he lacked in technique, so to speak. He now perceived that there was likely to be a miscarriage of justice here, and he rose to the occasion.

"Wait a moment, gentlemen," he said, "it is plain that an assault has been committed it is plain to anybody; but the way things are going, the guilty will certainly escape conviction. I can not allow this. Now——"

"But, your honor!" said Wilson, interrupting him, earnestly but respectfully, "you are deciding the case yourself, whereas the jury—"

"Never mind the jury, Mr. Wilson; the jury will have a chance when there is a reasonable doubt for them to take hold of—which there isn't, so far. There is no doubt whatever that an assault has been committed. The attempt to show that both of the accused committed it has failed. Are they both to escape justice on that account? Not in this court, if I can prevent it. It appears to have been a mistake to bring the charge against them as a corporation; each should have been charged in his capacity as an individual, and—"

"But, your honor!" said Wilson, "in fairness to my clients I must insist that inasmuch as the prosecution did not separate the—"

"No wrong will be done your clients, sir—they will be protected; also the public and the offended laws. Mr. Allen, you will amend your pleadings, and put one of the accused on trial at a time."

Wilson broke in: "But, your honor! this is wholly unprecedented! To imperil an accused person by arbitrarily altering and widening the charge against him in order to compass his conviction when the charge as originally brought promises to fail to convict, is a thing unheard of before."

"Unheard of where?"

"In the courts of this or any other state."

The judge said with dignity: "I am not acquainted with the customs of other courts, and am not concerned to know what they are. I am responsible for this court, and I cannot conscientiously allow my judgment to be warped and my judicial liberty hampered by trying to conform to the caprices of other courts, be they—"

"But, your honor, the oldest and highest courts in Europe—"

"This court is not run on the European plan, Mr. Wilson; it is not run on any plan but its own. It has a plan of its own; and that plan is, to find justice for both State and accused, no matter what happens to be practice and custom in Europe or anywhere else." (Great applause.) "Silence! It has not been the custom of this court to imitate other courts; it has not been the custom of this court to take shelter behind the decisions of other courts, and we will not begin now. We will do the best we can by the light that God has given us, and while this court continues to have His approval, it will remain indifferent to what other organizations may think of it." (Applause.) "Gentlemen, I must have order!—quiet yourselves! Mr. Allen, you will now proceed against the prisoners one at a time. Go on with the case."

Allen was not at his ease. However, after whispering a moment with his client and with one or two other people, he rose and said:

"Your honor, I find it to be reported and believed that the accused are able to act independently in many ways, but that this independence does not extend to their legs, authority over their legs being vested exclusively in the one brother during a specific term of days, and then passing to the other brother for a like term, and so on, by regular alternation. I could call witnesses who would prove that the accused had revealed to them the existence of this extraordinary fact, and had also made known which of them was in possession of the legs yesterday—and this would, of course, indicate where the guilt of the assault belongs—but as this would be mere hearsay evidence, these revelations not having been made under oath—"

"Never mind about that, Mr. Allen. It may not all be hearsay. We shall see. It may at least help to put us on the right track. Call the witnesses."

"Then I will call Mr. John Buckstone, who is now present, and I beg that Mrs. Patsy Cooper may be sent for. Take the stand, Mr. Buckstone."

Buckstone took the oath, and then testified that on the previous evening the Count Angelo Capello had protested against going to the hall, and had called all present to witness that he was going by compulsion and would not go if he could help himself. Also, that the Count Luigi had replied sharply that he would go, just the same, and that he, Count Luigi, would see to that himself. Also, that upon Count Angelo's complaining about being kept on his legs so long, Count Luigi retorted with apparent surprise, "Your legs!—I like your impudence!"

"Now we are getting at the kernel of the thing," observed the judge, with grave and earnest satisfaction. "It looks as if the Count Luigi was in possession of the battery at the time of the assault."

Nothing further was elicited from Mr. Buckstone on direct examination. Mr. Wilson took the witness.

"Mr. Buckstone, about what time was it that that conversation took place?"

"Toward nine yesterday evening, sir."

"Did you then proceed directly to the hall?"

"Yes, sir."

"How long did it take you to go there?"

"Well, we walked; and as it was from the extreme edge of the town, and there was no hurry, I judge it took us about twenty minutes, maybe a trifle more."

"About what hour was the kick delivered?"

"About thirteen minutes and a half to ten."

"Admirable! You are a pattern witness, Mr. Buckstone. How did you happen to look at your watch at that particular moment?"

"I always do it when I see an assault. It's likely I shall be called as a witness, and it's a good point to have."

"It would be well if others were as thoughtful. Was anything said, between the conversation at my house and the assault, upon the detail which we are now examining into?"

"No, sir."

"If power over the mutual legs was in the possession of one brother at nine, and passed into the possession of the other one during the next thirty or forty minutes, do you think you could have detected the change?"

"By no means!"

"That is all, Mr. Buckstone."

Mrs. Patsy Cooper was called. The crowd made way for her, and she came smiling and bowing through the narrow human lane, with Betsy Hale, as escort and support, smiling and bowing in her wake, the audience breaking into welcoming cheers as the old favorites filed along. The judge did not check this kindly demonstration of homage and affection, but let it run its course unrebuked.

The old ladies stopped and shook hands with the twins with effusion, then gave the judge a friendly nod, and bustled into the seats provided for them. They immediately began to deliver a volley of eager questions at the friends around them: "What is this thing for?" "What is that thing for?" "Who is that young man that's writing at the desk? Why, I declare, it's Jack Bunce! I thought he was sick." "Which is the jury? Why, is that the jury? Billy Price and Job Turner, and Jack Lounsbury, and—well, I never!" "Now who would ever 'a' thought—"

But they were gently called to order at this point, and asked not to talk in court. Their tongues fell silent, but the radiant interest in their faces remained, and their gratitude for the blessing of a new sensation and a novel experience still beamed undimmed from their eyes. Aunt Patsy stood up and took the oath, and Mr. Allen explained the point in issue, and asked her to go on now, in her own way, and throw as much light upon it as she could. She toyed with her reticule a moment or two, as if considering where to begin, then she said:

"Well, the way of it is this. They are Luigi's legs a week at a time, and then they are Angelo's, and he can do whatever he wants to with them."

"You are making a mistake, Aunt Patsy Cooper," said the judge. "You shouldn't state that as a fact, because you don't know it to be a fact."

"What's the reason I don't?" said Aunt Patsy, bridling a little.

"What is the reason that you do know it?"

"The best in the world because they told me."

"That isn't a reason."

"Well, for the land's sake! Betsy Hale, do you hear that?"

"Hear it? I should think so," said Aunt Betsy, rising and facing the court. "Why, Judge, I was there and heard it myself. Luigi says to Angelo—no, it was Angelo said it to—"

"Come, come, Mrs. Hale, pray sit down, and—"

"Certainly, it's all right, I'm going to sit down presently, but not until I've—"

"But you must sit down!"

"Must! Well, upon my word if things ain't getting to a pretty pass when—"

The house broke into laughter, but was promptly brought to order, and meantime Mr. Allen persuaded the old lady to take her seat. Aunt Patsy continued:

"Yes, they told me that, and I know it's true. They're Luigi's legs this week, but—"

"Ah, they told you that, did they?" said the Justice, with interest.

51

"Well, no, I don't know that they told me, but that's neither here nor there. I know, without that, that at dinner yesterday, Angelo was as tired as a dog, and yet Luigi wouldn't lend him the legs to go up-stairs and take a nap with."

"Did he ask for them?"

"Let me see—it seems to me, somehow, that—that—Aunt Betsy, do you remember whether he—"

"Never mind about what Aunt Betsy remembers—she is not a witness; we only want to know what YOU remember yourself," said the judge.

"Well, it does seem to me that you are most cantankerously particular about a little thing, Sim Robinson. Why, when I can't remember a thing myself, I always—"

"Ah, please go on!"

"Now how can she when you keep fussing at her all the time?" said Aunt Betsy. "Why, with a person pecking at me that way, I should get that fuzzled and fuddled that—"

She was on her feet again, but Allen coaxed her into her seat once more, while the court squelched the mirth of the house. Then the judge said:

"Madam, do you know—do you absolutely know, independently of anything these gentlemen have told you—that the power over their legs passes from the one to the other regularly every week?"

"Regularly? Bless your heart, regularly ain't any name for the exactness of it! All the big cities in Europe used to set the clocks by it." (Laughter, suppressed by the court.)

"How do you know? That is the question. Please answer it plainly and squarely."

"Don't you talk to me like that, Sim Robinson—I won't have it. How do I know, indeed! How do YOU know what you know? Because somebody told you. You didn't invent it out of your own head, did you? Why, these twins are the truthfulest people in the world; and I don't think it becomes you to sit up there and throw slurs at them when they haven't been doing anything to you. And they are orphans besides—both of them. All—"

But Aunt Betsy was up again now, and both old ladies were talking at once and with all their might; but as the house was weltering in a storm of laughter, and the judge was hammering his desk with an iron paper-weight, one could only see them talk, not hear them. At last, when quiet was restored, the court said:

"Let the ladies retire."

"But, your honor, I have the right, in the interest of my clients,—to cross-exam—"

"You'll not need to exercise it, Mr. Wilson—the evidence is thrown out."

"Thrown out!" said Aunt Patsy, ruffled; "and what's it thrown out for, I'd like to know."

"And so would I, Patsy Cooper. It seems to me that if we can save these poor persecuted strangers, it is our bounden duty to stand up here and talk for them till—"

"There, there, there, do sit down!"

It cost some trouble and a good deal of coaxing, but they were got into their seats at last. The trial was soon ended now. The twins themselves became witnesses in their own defense. They established the fact, upon oath, that the leg-power passed from one to the other every Saturday night at twelve o'clock sharp. But on cross-examination their counsel would not allow them to tell whose week of power the current week was. The judge insisted upon their answering, and proposed to compel them, but even the prosecution took fright and came to the rescue then, and helped stay the sturdy jurist's revolutionary hand. So the case had to go to the jury with that important point hanging in the air. They were out an hour and brought in this verdict:

"We the jury do find: 1, that an assault was committed, as charged; 2, that it was committed by one of the persons accused, he having been seen to do it by several credible witnesses; 3, but that his identity is so merged in his brother's that we have not been able to tell which was him. We cannot convict both, for only one is guilty. We cannot acquit both, for only one is innocent. Our verdict is that justice has been defeated by the dispensation of God, and ask to be discharged from further duty."

This was read aloud in court and brought out a burst of hearty applause. The old ladies made a spring at the twins, to shake and congratulate, but were gently disengaged by Mr. Wilson and softly crowded back into their places.

The judge rose in his little tribune, laid aside his silver-bowed spectacles, roached his gray hair up with his fingers, and said, with dignity and solemnity, and even with a certain pathos:

"In all my experience on the bench, I have not seen justice bow her head in shame in this court until this day. You little realize what far-reaching harm has just been wrought here under the fickle forms of law. Imitation is the bane of courts—I thank God that this one is free from the contamination of that vice—and in no long time you will see the fatal work of this hour seized upon by profligate so-called guardians of justice in all the wide circumstance of this planet and perpetuated in their pernicious decisions. I wash my hands of this iniquity. I would have compelled these culprits to expose their guilt, but support failed me where I had most right to expect aid and encouragement. And I was confronted by a law made in the interest of crime, which protects the criminal from testifying against himself. Yet I had precedents of my own whereby I had set aside that law on two different occasions and thus succeeded in convicting criminals to whose crimes there were no witnesses but themselves. What have you accomplished this day? Do you realize it? You have set adrift, unadmonished, in this community, two men endowed with an awful and mysterious gift, a hidden and grisly power for evil—a power by which each in his turn may commit crime after crime of the most heinous character, and no man be able to tell which is the guilty or which the innocent party in any case of them all. Look to your homes—look to your property— look to your lives—for you have need!

"Prisoners at the bar, stand up. Through suppression of evidence, a jury of your—our—countrymen have been obliged to deliver a verdict concerning your case which stinks to heaven with the rankness of its injustice. By its terms you, the guilty one, go free with the innocent. Depart in peace, and come no more! The costs devolve upon the outraged plaintiff—another iniquity. The court stands dissolved."

Almost everybody crowded forward to overwhelm the twins and their counsel with congratulations; but presently the two old aunties dug the duplicates out and bore them away in triumph through the hurrahing crowd, while lots of new friends carried Pudd'nhead Wilson off tavern-ward to feast him and "wet down" his great and victorious entry into the legal arena. To Wilson, so long familiar with neglect and depreciation, this strange new incense of popularity and admiration was as a fragrance blown from the fields of paradise. A happy man was Wilson.

CHAPTER VI. THE AMAZING DUEL

A deputation came in the evening and conferred upon Wilson the welcome honor of a nomination for mayor; for the village has just been converted into a city by charter. Tom skulks out of challenging the twins. Judge Driscoll thereupon challenges Angelo (accused by Tom of doing the kicking); he declines, but Luigi accepts in his place against Angelo's timid protest.

It was late Saturday night nearing eleven.

The judge and his second found the rest of the war party at the further end of the vacant ground, near the haunted house. Pudd'nhead Wilson advanced to meet them, and said anxiously:

"I must say a word in behalf of my principal's proxy, Count Luigi, to whom you have kindly granted the privilege of fighting my principal's battle for him. It is growing late, and Count Luigi is in great trouble lest midnight shall strike before the finish."

"It is another testimony," said Howard, approvingly. "That young man is fine all through. He wishes to save his brother the sorrow of fighting on the Sabbath, and he is right; it is the right and manly feeling and does him credit. We will make all possible haste."

Wilson said: "There is also another reason—a consideration, in fact, which deeply concerns Count Luigi himself. These twins have command of their mutual legs turn about. Count Luigi is in command now; but at midnight, possession will pass to my principal, Count Angelo, and—well, you can foresee what will happen. He will march straight off the field, and carry Luigi with him."

"Why! sure enough!" cried the judge, "we have heard something about that extraordinary law of their being, already—nothing very definite, it is true, as regards dates and durations of power, but I see it is definite enough as regards to-night. Of course we must give Luigi every chance. Omit all the ceremonial possible, gentlemen, and place us in position."

The seconds at once tossed up a coin; Howard won the choice. He placed the judge sixty feet from the haunted house and facing it; Wilson placed the twins within fifteen feet of the house and facing the judge—necessarily. The pistol-case was opened and the long slim tubes taken out; when the moonlight glinted from them a shiver went through Angelo. The doctor was a fool, but a thoroughly well-meaning one, with a kind heart and a sincere disposition to oblige, but along with it an absence of tact which often hurt its effectiveness. He brought his box of lint and bandages, and asked Angelo to feel and see how soft and comfortable they were. Angelo's head fell over against Luigi's in a faint, and precious time was lost in bringing him to; which provoked Luigi into expressing his mind to the doctor with a good deal of vigor and frankness. After Angelo came to he was still so weak that Luigi was obliged to drink a stiff horn of brandy to brace him up.

The seconds now stepped at once to their posts, halfway between the combatants, one of them on each side of the line of fire. Wilson was to count, very deliberately, "One-two-three-fire!—stop!" and the duelists could bang away at any time they chose during that recitation, but not after the last word. Angelo grew very nervous when he saw Wilson's hand rising slowly into the air as a sign to make ready, and he leaned his head against Luigi's and said:

"Oh, please take me away from here, I can't stay, I know I can't!"

"What in the world are you doing? Straighten up! What's the matter with you?—you're in no danger—nobody's going to shoot at you. Straighten up, I tell you!"

Angelo obeyed, just in time to hear:

"One—!"

"Bang!" Just one report, and a little tuft of white hair floated slowly to the judge's feet in the moonlight. The judge did not swerve; he still stood erect and motionless, like a statue, with his pistol-arm hanging straight down at his side. He was reserving his fire.

"Two—!"

"Three—"!

"Fire—!"

Up came the pistol-arm instantly-Angelo dodged with the report. He said "Ouch!" and fainted again.

The doctor examined and bandaged the wound.

It was of no consequence, he said—bullet through fleshy part of arm—no bones broken—the gentleman was still able to fight let the duel proceed.

Next time Angelo jumped just as Luigi fired, which disordered his aim and caused him to cut a chip off of Howard's ear. The judge took his time again, and when he fired Angelo jumped and got a knuckle skinned. The doctor inspected and dressed the wounds. Angelo now spoke out and said he was content with the satisfaction he had got, and if the judge—but Luigi shut him roughly up, and asked him not to make an ass of himself; adding:

"And I want you to stop dodging. You take a great deal too prominent a part in this thing for a person who has got nothing to do with it. You should remember that you are here only by courtesy, and are without official recognition; officially you are not here at all; officially you do not even exist. To all intents and purposes you are absent from this place, and you ought for your own modesty's sake to reflect that it cannot become a person who is not present here to be taking this sort of public and indecent prominence in a matter in which he is not in the slightest degree concerned. Now, don't dodge again; the bullets are not for you, they are for me; if I want them dodged I will attend to it myself. I never saw a person act so."

Angelo saw the reasonableness of what his brother had said, and he did try to reform, but it was of no use; both pistols went off at the same instant, and he jumped once more; he got a sharp scrape along his cheek from the judge's bullet, and so deflected Luigi's aim that his ball went wide and chipped a flake of skin from Pudd'nhead Wilson's chin. The doctor attended to the wounded.

By the terms, the duel was over. But Luigi was entirely out of patience, and begged for one more exchange of shots, insisting that he had had no fair chance, on account of his brother's indelicate behavior. Howard was opposed to granting so unusual a privilege, but the judge took Luigi's part, and added that indeed he himself might fairly be considered entitled to another trial, because although the proxy on the other side was in no way to blame for his (the judge's) humiliatingly resultless work, the gentleman with whom he was fighting this duel was to blame for it, since if he had played no advantages and had held his head still, his proxy would have been disposed of early. He added:

"Count Luigi's request for another exchange is another proof that he is a brave and chivalrous gentleman, and I beg that the courtesy he asks may be accorded him."

"I thank you most sincerely for this generosity, Judge Driscoll," said Luigi, with a polite bow, and moving to his place. Then he added—to Angelo, "Now hold your grip, hold your grip, I tell you, and I'll land him sure!"

The men stood erect, their pistol-arms at their sides, the two seconds stood at their official posts, the doctor stood five paces in Wilson's rear with his instruments and bandages in his hands. The deep stillness, the peaceful moonlight, the motionless figures, made an impressive picture and the impending fatal possibilities augmented this impressiveness to solemnity. Wilson's hand began to rise—slowly—slowly—higher—still higher—still higher—in another moment:

"Boom!" the first stroke of midnight swung up out of the distance; Angelo was off like a deer!

"Oh, you unspeakable traitor!" wailed his brother, as they went soaring over the fence.

The others stood astonished and gazing; and so stood, watching that strange spectacle until distance dissolved it and swept it from their view. Then they rubbed their eyes like people waking out of a dream.

"Well, I've never seen anything like that before!" said the judge. "Wilson, I am going to confess now, that I wasn't quite able to believe in that leg business, and had a suspicion that it was a put-up convenience between those twins; and when Count Angelo fainted I thought I saw the whole scheme—thought it was pretext No. 1, and would be followed by others till twelve o'clock should arrive, and Luigi would get off with all the credit of seeming to want to fight and yet not have to fight, after all. But I was mistaken. His pluck proved it. He's a brave fellow and did want to fight."

"There isn't any doubt about that," said Howard, and added, in a grieved tone, "but what an unworthy sort of Christian that Angelo is—I hope and believe there are not many like him. It is not right to engage in a duel on the Sabbath—I could not approve of that myself; but to finish one that has been begun—that is a duty, let the day be what it may."

They strolled along, still wondering, still talking.

"It is a curious circumstance," remarked the surgeon, halting Wilson a moment to paste some more court-plaster on his chin, which had gone to leaking blood again, "that in this duel neither of the parties who handled the pistols lost blood while nearly all the persons present in the mere capacity of guests got hit. I have not heard of such a thing before. Don't you think it unusual?"

"Yes," said the Judge, "it has struck me as peculiar. Peculiar and unfortunate. I was annoyed at it, all the time. In the case of Angelo it made no great difference, because he was in a measure concerned, though not officially; but it troubled me to see the seconds compromised, and yet I knew no way to mend the matter.

"There was no way to mend it," said Howard, whose ear was being readjusted now by the doctor; "the code fixes our place, and it would not have been lawful to change it. If we could have stood at your side, or behind you, or in front of you, it—but it would not have been legitimate and the other parties would have had a just right to complain of our trying to protect ourselves from danger; infractions of the code are certainly not permissible in any case whatever."

Wilson offered no remarks. It seemed to him that there was very little place here for so much solemnity, but he judged that if a duel where nobody was in danger or got crippled but the seconds and the outsiders had nothing ridiculous about it for these gentlemen, his pointing out that feature would probably not help them to see it.

He invited them in to take a nightcap, and Howard and the judge accepted, but the doctor said he would have to go and see how Angelo's principal wound was getting on.

> [It was now Sunday, and in the afternoon Angelo was to be received into the Baptist communion by immersion—a doubtful prospect, the doctor feared.]

CHAPTER VII. LUIGI DEFIES GALEN

When the doctor arrived at Aunt Patsy Cooper's house, he found the lights going and everybody up and dressed and in a great state of solicitude and excitement. The twins were stretched on a sofa in the sitting-room, Aunt Patsy was fussing at Angelo's arm, Nancy was flying around under her commands, the two young boys were trying to keep out of the way and always getting in it, in order to see and wonder, Rowena stood apart, helpless with apprehension and emotion, and Luigi was growling in unappeasable fury over Angelo's shameful flight.

As has been reported before, the doctor was a fool—a kind-hearted and well-meaning one, but with no tact; and as he was by long odds the most learned physician in the town, and was quite well aware of it, and could talk his learning with ease and precision, and liked to show off when he had an audience, he was sometimes tempted into revealing more of a case than was good for the patient.

He examined Angelo's wound, and was really minded to say nothing for once; but Aunt Patsy was so anxious and so pressing that he allowed his caution to be overcome, and proceeded to empty himself as follows, with scientific relish:

"Without going too much into detail, madam—for you would probably not understand it, anyway—I concede that great care is going to be necessary here; otherwise exudation of the esophagus is nearly sure to ensue, and this will be followed by ossification and extradition of the maxillaris superioris, which must decompose the granular surfaces of the great infusorial ganglionic system, thus obstructing the action of the posterior varioloid arteries, and precipitating compound strangulated sorosis of the valvular tissues, and ending unavoidably in the dispersion and combustion of the marsupial fluxes and the consequent embrocation of the bicuspid populo redax referendum rotulorum."

A miserable silence followed. Aunt Patsy's heart sank, the pallor of despair invaded her face, she was not able to speak; poor Rowena wrung her hands in privacy and silence, and said to herself in the bitterness of her young grief, "There is no hope—it is plain there is no hope"; the good-hearted negro wench, Nancy, paled to chocolate, then to orange, then to amber, and thought to herself with yearning sympathy and sorrow, "Po' thing, he ain' gwyne to las' throo de half o' dat"; small Henry choked up, and turned his head away to hide his rising tears, and his brother Joe said to himself, with a sense of loss, "The baptizing's busted, that's sure." Luigi was the only person who had any heart to speak. He said, a little bit sharply, to the doctor:

"Well, well, there's nothing to be gained by wasting precious time; give him a barrel of pills—I'll take them for him."

"You?" asked the doctor.

"Yes. Did you suppose he was going to take them himself?"

"Why, of course."

"Well, it's a mistake. He never took a dose of medicine in his life. He can't."

"Well, upon my word, it's the most extraordinary thing I ever heard of!"

"Oh," said Aunt Patsy, as pleased as a mother whose child is being admired and wondered at; "you'll find that there's more about them that's wonderful than their just being made in the image of God like the rest of His creatures, now you can depend on that, I tell you," and she wagged her complacent head like one who could reveal marvelous things if she chose.

The boy Joe began:

"Why, ma, they ain't made in the im—"

"You shut up, and wait till you're asked, Joe. I'll let you know when I want help. Are you looking for something, doctor?"

The doctor asked for a few sheets of paper and a pen, and said he would write a prescription; which he did. It was one of Galen's; in fact, it was Galen's favorite, and had been slaying people for sixteen thousand years. Galen used it for everything, applied it to everything, said it would remove everything, from warts all the way through to lungs and it generally did. Galen was still the only medical authority recognized in Missouri; his practice was the only practice known to the Missouri doctors, and his prescriptions were the only ammunition they carried when they went out for game.

By and by Dr. Claypool laid down his pen and read the result of his labors aloud, carefully and deliberately, for this battery must be constructed on the premises by the family, and mistakes could occur; for he wrote a doctor's hand—the hand which from the beginning of time has been so disastrous to the apothecary and so profitable to the undertaker:

"Take of afarabocca, henbane, corpobalsamum, each two drams and a half; of cloves, opium, myrrh, cyperus, each two drams; of opobalsamum, Indian leaf, cinnamon, zedoary, ginger, coftus, coral, cassia, euphorbium, gum tragacanth, frankincense, styrax calamita, Celtic, nard, spignel, hartwort, mustard, saxifrage, dill, anise, each one dram; of xylaloes, rheum ponticum, alipta, moschata, castor, spikenard, galangals, opoponax, anacardium, mastich, brimstone, peony, eringo, pulp of dates, red and white hermodactyls, roses, thyme, acorns, pennyroyal, gentian, the bark of the root of mandrake, germander, valerian, bishop's-weed, bayberries, long and white pepper, xylobalsamum, carnabadium, macedonian, parsley seeds, lovage, the seeds of rue, and sinon, of each a dram and a half; of pure gold, pure silver, pearls not perforated, the blatta byzantina, the bone of the stag's heart, of each the quantity of fourteen grains of wheat; of sapphire, emerald and jasper stones, each one dram; of hazel-nuts, two drams; of pellitory of Spain, shavings of ivory, calamus odoratus, each the quantity of twenty-nine grains of wheat; of honey or sugar a sufficient quantity. Boil down and skim off."

"There," he said, "that will fix the patient; give his brother a dipperful every three-quarters of an hour—"

"—while he survives," muttered Luigi—

"—and see that the room is kept wholesomely hot, and the doors and windows closed tight. Keep Count Angelo nicely covered up with six or seven blankets, and when he is thirsty—which will be frequently—moisten a rag in the vapor of the tea kettle and let his brother suck it. When he is hungry—which will also be frequently—he must not be humored oftener than every seven or eight hours; then toast part of a cracker until it begins to brown, and give it to his brother."

"That is all very well, as far as Angelo is concerned," said Luigi, "but what am I to eat?"

"I do not see that there is anything the matter with you," the doctor answered, "you may, of course, eat what you please."

"And also drink what I please, I suppose?"

"Oh, certainly—at present. When the violent and continuous perspiring has reduced your strength, I shall have to reduce your diet, of course, and also bleed you, but there is no occasion for that yet awhile." He turned to Aunt Patsy and said: "He must be put to bed, and sat up with, and tended with the greatest care, and not allowed to stir for several days and nights."

"For one, I'm sacredly thankful for that," said Luigi, "it postpones the funeral—I'm not to be drowned to-day, anyhow."

Angelo said quietly to the doctor:

"I will cheerfully submit to all your requirements, sir, up to two o'clock this afternoon, and will resume them after three, but cannot be confined to the house during that intermediate hour."

"Why, may I ask?"

"Because I have entered the Baptist communion, and by appointment am to be baptised in the river at that hour."

"Oh, insanity!—it cannot be allowed!"

Angelo answered with placid firmness:

"Nothing shall prevent it, if I am alive."

"Why, consider, my dear sir, in your condition it might prove fatal."

A tender and ecstatic smile beamed from Angelo's eyes, and he broke forth in a tone of joyous fervency:

"Ah, how blessed it would be to die for such a cause—it would be martyrdom!"

"But your brother—consider your brother; you would be risking his life, too."

"He risked mine an hour ago," responded Angelo, gloomily; "did he consider me?" A thought swept through his mind that made him shudder. "If I had not run, I might have been killed in a duel on the Sabbath day, and my soul would have been lost—lost."

"Oh, don't fret, it wasn't in any danger," said Luigi, irritably; "they wouldn't waste it for a little thing like that; there's a glass case all ready for it in the heavenly museum, and a pin to stick it up with."

Aunt Patsy was shocked, and said:

"Looy, Looy!—don't talk so, dear!"

Rowena's soft heart was pierced by Luigi's unfeeling words, and she murmured to herself, "Oh, if I but had the dear privilege of protecting and defending him with my weak voice!—but alas! this sweet boon is denied me by the cruel conventions of social intercourse."

"Get their bed ready," said Aunt Patsy to Nancy, "and shut up the windows and doors, and light their candles, and see that you drive all the mosquitoes out of their bar, and make up a good fire in their stove, and carry up some bags of hot ashes to lay to his feet—"

"—and a shovel of fire for his head, and a mustard plaster for his neck, and some gum shoes for his ears," Luigi interrupted, with temper; and added, to himself, "Damnation, I'm going to be roasted alive, I just know it!"

"Why, Looy! Do be quiet; I never saw such a fractious thing. A body would think you didn't care for your brother."

"I don't—to that extent, Aunt Patsy. I was glad the drowning was postponed a minute ago, but I'm not now. No, that is all gone by; I want to be drowned."

"You'll bring a judgment on yourself just as sure as you live, if you go on like that. Why, I never heard the beat of it. Now, there—there! you've said enough. Not another word out of you—I won't have it!"

"But, Aunt Patsy—"

"Luigi! Didn't you hear what I told you?"

"But, Aunt Patsy, I—why, I'm not going to set my heart and lungs afloat in that pail of sewage which this criminal here has been prescri—"

"Yes, you are, too. You are going to be good, and do everything I tell you, like a dear," and she tapped his cheek affectionately with her finger. "Rowena, take the prescription and go in the kitchen and hunt up the things and lay them out for me. I'll sit up with my patient the rest of the night, doctor; I can't trust Nancy, she couldn't make Luigi take the medicine. Of course, you'll drop in again during the day. Have you got any more directions?"

"No, I believe not, Aunt Patsy. If I don't get in earlier, I'll be along by early candle-light, anyway. Meantime, don't allow him to get out of his bed."

Angelo said, with calm determination:

"I shall be baptized at two o'clock. Nothing but death shall prevent me."

The doctor said nothing aloud, but to himself he said:

"Why, this chap's got a manly side, after all! Physically he's a coward, but morally he's a lion. I'll go and tell the others about this; it will raise him a good deal in their estimation—and the public will follow their lead, of course."

Privately, Aunt Patsy applauded too, and was proud of Angelo's courage in the moral field as she was of Luigi's in the field of honor.

The boy Henry was troubled, but the boy Joe said, inaudibly, and gratefully, "We're all honky, after all; and no postponement on account of the weather."

CHAPTER VIII. BAPTISM OF THE BETTER HALF

By nine o'clock the town was humming with the news of the midnight duel, and there were but two opinions about it: one, that Luigi's pluck in the field was most praiseworthy and Angelo's flight most scandalous; the other, that Angelo's courage in flying the field for conscience' sake was as fine and creditable as was Luigi's in holding the field in the face of the bullets. The one opinion was held by half of the town, the other one was maintained by the other half. The division was clean and exact, and it made two parties, an Angelo party and a Luigi party. The twins had suddenly become popular idols along with Pudd'nhead Wilson, and haloed with a glory as intense as his. The children talked the duel all the way to Sunday-school, their elders talked it all the way to church, the choir discussed it behind their red curtain, it usurped the place of pious thought in the "nigger gallery."

By noon the doctor had added the news, and spread it, that Count Angelo, in spite of his wound and all warnings and supplications, was resolute in his determination to be baptized at the hour appointed. This swept the town like wildfire, and mightily reinforced the enthusiasm of the Angelo faction, who said, "If any doubted that it was moral courage that took him from the field, what have they to say now!"

Still the excitement grew. All the morning it was traveling countryward, toward all points of the compass; so, whereas before only the farmers and their wives were intending to come and witness the remarkable baptism, a general holiday was now proclaimed and the children and negroes admitted to the privileges of the occasion. All the farms for ten miles around were vacated, all the converging roads emptied long processions of wagons, horses, and yeomanry into the town. The pack and cram of people vastly exceeded any that had ever been seen in that sleepy region before. The only thing that had ever even approached it, was the time long gone by, but never forgotten, nor even referred to without wonder and pride, when two circuses and a Fourth of July fell together. But the glory of that occasion was extinguished now for good. It was but a freshet to this deluge.

The great invasion massed itself on the river-bank and waited hungrily for the immense event. Waited, and wondered if it would really happen, or if the twin who was not a "professor" would stand out and prevent it.

But they were not to be disappointed. Angelo was as good as his word. He came attended by an escort of honor composed of several hundred of the best citizens, all of the Angelo party; and when the immersion was finished they escorted him back home and would even have carried him on their shoulders, but that people might think they were carrying Luigi.

Far into the night the citizens continued to discuss and wonder over the strangely mated pair of incidents that had distinguished and exalted the past twenty-four hours above any other twenty-four in the history of their town for picturesqueness and splendid interest; and long before the lights were out and burghers asleep it had been decided on all hands that in capturing these twins Dawson's Landing had drawn a prize in the great lottery of municipal fortune.

At midnight Angelo was sleeping peacefully. His immersion had not harmed him, it had merely made him wholesomely drowsy, and he had been dead asleep many hours now. It had made Luigi drowsy, too, but he had got only brief naps, on account of his having to take the medicine every three-quarters of an hour-and Aunt Betsy Hale was there to see that he did it. When he complained and resisted, she was quietly firm with him, and said in a low voice:

"No-no, that won't do; you mustn't talk, and you mustn't retch and gag that way, either—you'll wake up your poor brother."

"Well, what of it, Aunt Betsy, he—"

"'Sh-h! Don't make a noise dear. You mustn't forget that your poor brother is sick and—"

"Sick, is he? Well, I wish I—"

"'Sh-h-h! Will you be quiet, Luigi! Here, now, take the rest of it—don't keep me holding the dipper all night. I declare if you haven't left a good fourth of it in the bottom! Come—that's a good—

"Aunt Betsy, don't make me! I feel like I've swallowed a cemetery; I do, indeed. Do let me rest a little—just a little; I can't take any more of the devilish stuff now."

"Luigi! Using such language here, and him just baptized! Do you want the roof to fall on you?"

"I wish to goodness it would!"

"Why, you dreadful thing! I've a good notion to—let that blanket alone; do you want your brother to catch his death?"

"Aunt Betsy, I've got to have it off, I'm being roasted alive; nobody could stand it—you couldn't yourself."

"Now, then, you're sneezing again—I just expected it."

"Because I've caught a cold in my head. I always do, when I go in the water with my clothes on. And it takes me weeks to get over it, too. I think it was a shame to serve me so."

"Luigi, you are unreasonable; you know very well they couldn't baptize him dry. I should think you would be willing to undergo a little inconvenience for your brother's sake."

"Inconvenience! Now how you talk, Aunt Betsy. I came as near as anything to getting drowned you saw that yourself; and do you call this inconvenience?—the room shut up as tight as a drum, and so hot the mosquitoes are trying to get out; and a cold in the head, and dying for sleep and no chance to get any—on account of this infamous medicine that that assassin prescri—"

"There, you're sneezing again. I'm going down and mix some more of this truck for you, dear."

CHAPTER IX. THE DRINKLESS DRUNK

During Monday, Tuesday, and Wednesday the twins grew steadily worse; but then the doctor was summoned South to attend his mother's funeral, and they got well in forty-eight hours. They appeared on the street on Friday, and were welcomed with enthusiasm by the new-born parties, the Luigi and Angelo factions. The Luigi faction carried its strength into the Democratic party, the Angelo faction entered into a combination with the Whigs. The Democrats nominated Luigi for alderman under the new city government, and the Whigs put up Angelo against him. The Democrats nominated Pudd'nhead Wilson for mayor, and he was left alone in this glory, for the Whigs had no man who was willing to enter the lists against such a formidable opponent. No politician had scored such a compliment as this before in the history of the Mississippi Valley.

The political campaign in Dawson's Landing opened in a pretty warm fashion, and waxed hotter every week. Luigi's whole heart was in it, and even Angelo developed a surprising amount of interest-which was natural, because he was not merely representing Whigism, a matter of no consequence to him; but he was representing something immensely finer and greater—to wit, Reform. In him was centered the hopes of the whole reform element of the town; he was the chosen and admired champion of every clique that had a pet reform of any sort or kind at heart. He was president of the great Teetotalers' Union, its chiefest prophet and mouthpiece.

But as the canvass went on, troubles began to spring up all around—troubles for the twins, and through them for all the parties and segments and fractions of parties. Whenever Luigi had possession of the legs, he carried Angelo to balls, rum shops, Sons of Liberty parades, horse-races, campaign riots, and everywhere else that could damage him with his party and the church; and when it was Angelo's week he carried Luigi diligently to all manner of moral and religious gatherings, doing his best to regain the ground he had lost before. As a result of these double performances, there was a storm blowing all the time, an ever-rising storm, too—a storm of frantic criticism of the twins, and rage over their extravagant, incomprehensible conduct.

Luigi had the final chance. The legs were his for the closing week of the canvass. He led his brother a fearful dance.

But he saved his best card for the very eve of the election. There was to be a grand turnout of the Teetotalers' Union that day, and Angelo was to march at the head of the procession and deliver a great oration afterward. Luigi drank a couple of glasses of whisky—which steadied his nerves and clarified his mind, but made Angelo drunk. Everybody who saw the march, saw that the Champion of the Teetotalers was half seas over, and noted also that his brother, who made no hypocritical pretensions to extra temperance virtues, was dignified and sober. This eloquent fact could not be unfruitful at the end of a hot political canvass. At the mass-meeting Angelo tried to make his great temperance oration, but was so discommoded—by hiccoughs and thickness of tongue that he had to give it up; then drowsiness overtook him and his head drooped against Luigi's and he went to sleep. Luigi apologized for him, and was going on to improve his opportunity with an appeal for a moderation of what he called "the prevailing teetotal madness," but persons in the audience began to howl and throw things at him, and then the meeting rose in wrath and chased him home.

This episode was a crusher for Angelo in another way. It destroyed his chances with Rowena. Those chances had been growing, right along, for two months. Rowena had partly confessed that she loved him, but wanted time to consider. Now the tender dream was ended, and she told him so the moment he was sober enough to understand. She said she would never marry a man who drank.

"But I don't drink," he pleaded.

"That is nothing to the point," she said, coldly, "you get drunk, and that is worse."

[There was a long and sufficiently idiotic discussion here, which ended as reported in a previous note.]

CHAPTER X. SO THEY HANGED LUIGI

Dawson's Landing had a week of repose, after the election, and it needed it, for the frantic and variegated nightmare which had tormented it all through the preceding week had left it limp, haggard, and exhausted at the end. It got the week of repose because Angelo had the legs, and was in too subdued a condition to want to go out and mingle with an irritated community that had come to distrust and detest him because there was such a lack of harmony between his morals, which were confessedly excellent, and his methods of illustrating them, which were distinctly damnable. The new city officers were sworn in on the following Monday—at least all but Luigi. There was a complication in his case. His election was conceded, but he could not sit in the board of aldermen without his brother, and his brother could not sit there because he was not a member. There seemed to be no way out of the difficulty but to carry the matter into the courts, so this was resolved upon.

The case was set for the Monday fortnight. In due course the time arrived. In the mean time the city government had been at a standstill, because without Luigi there was a tie in the board of aldermen, whereas with him the liquor interest—the richest in the political field—would have one majority. But the court decided that Angelo could not sit in the board with him, either in public or executive sessions, and at the same time forbade the board to deny admission to Luigi, a fairly and legally chosen alderman. The case was carried up and up from court to court, yet still the same old original decision was confirmed every time. As a result, the city government not only stood still, with its hands tied, but everything it was created to protect and care for went a steady gait toward rack and ruin. There was no way to levy a tax, so the minor officials had to resign or starve; therefore they resigned. There being no city money, the enormous legal expenses on both sides had to be defrayed by private subscription. But at last the people came to their senses, and said:

"Pudd'nhead was right at the start—we ought to have hired the official half of that human phillipene to resign; but it's too late now; some of us haven't got anything left to hire him with."

"Yes, we have," said another citizen, "we've got this"—and he produced a halter.

Many shouted: "That's the ticket." But others said: "No—Count Angelo is innocent; we mustn't hang him."

"Who said anything about hanging him? We are only going to hang the other one."

"Then that is all right—there is no objection to that."

So they hanged Luigi. And so ends the history of "Those Extraordinary Twins."

FINAL REMARKS

As you see, it was an extravagant sort of a tale, and had no purpose but to exhibit that monstrous "freak" in all sorts of grotesque lights. But when Roxy wandered into the tale she had to be furnished with something to do; so she changed the children in the cradle; this necessitated the invention of a reason for it; this, in turn, resulted in making the children prominent personages—nothing could prevent it of course. Their career began to take a tragic aspect, and some one had to be brought in to help work the machinery; so Pudd'nhead Wilson was introduced and taken on trial. By this time the whole show was being run by the new people and in their interest, and the original show was become side-tracked and forgotten; the twin-monster, and the heroine, and the lads, and the old ladies had dwindled to inconsequentialities and were merely in the way. Their story was one story, the new people's story was another story, and there was no connection between them, no interdependence, no kinship. It is not practicable or rational to try to tell two stories at the same time; so I dug out the farce and left the tragedy.

The reader already knew how the expert works; he knows now how the other kind do it.

MARK TWAIN.

About Author

Samuel Langhorne Clemens (November 30, 1835 – April 21, 1910), known by his pen name Mark Twain, was an American writer, humorist, entrepreneur, publisher, and lecturer. He was lauded as the "greatest humorist this country has produced", and William Faulkner called him "the father of American literature". His novels include The Adventures of Tom Sawyer (1876) and its sequel, the Adventures of Huckleberry Finn (1884), the latter often called "The Great American Novel".

Twain was raised in Hannibal, Missouri, which later provided the setting for Tom Sawyer and Huckleberry Finn. He served an apprenticeship with a printer and then worked as a typesetter, contributing articles to the newspaper of his older brother Orion Clemens. He later became a riverboat pilot on the Mississippi River before heading west to join Orion in Nevada. He referred humorously to his lack of success at mining, turning to journalism for the Virginia City Territorial Enterprise. His humorous story, "The Celebrated Jumping Frog of Calaveras County", was published in 1865, based on a story that he heard at Angels Hotel in Angels Camp, California, where he had spent some time as a miner. The short story brought international attention and was even translated into French. His wit and satire, in prose and in speech, earned praise from critics and peers, and he was a friend to presidents, artists, industrialists, and European royalty.

Twain earned a great deal of money from his writings and lectures, but he invested in ventures that lost most of it—such as the Paige Compositor, a mechanical typesetter that failed because of its complexity and imprecision. He filed for bankruptcy in the wake of these financial setbacks, but he eventually overcame his financial troubles with the help of Henry Huttleston Rogers. He eventually paid all his creditors in full, even though his bankruptcy relieved him of having to do so.

Twain was born shortly after an appearance of Halley's Comet, and he predicted that he would "go out with it" as well; he died the day after the comet returned.

Biography

Early life

Samuel Langhorne Clemens was born on November 30, 1835, in Florida, Missouri, the sixth of seven children born to Jane (née Lampton; 1803–1890), a native of Kentucky, and John Marshall Clemens (1798–1847), a native of Virginia. His parents met when his father moved to Missouri, and they were married in 1823. Twain was of Cornish, English, and Scots-Irish descent. Only three of his siblings survived childhood: Orion (1825–1897), Henry (1838–1858), and Pamela (1827–1904). His sister Margaret (1830–1839) died when Twain was three, and his brother Benjamin (1832–1842) died three years later. His brother Pleasant Hannibal (1828) died at three weeks of age.

When he was four, Twain's family moved to Hannibal, Missouri, a port town on the Mississippi River that inspired the fictional town of St. Petersburg in The Adventures of Tom Sawyer and the Adventures of Huckleberry Finn. Slavery was legal in Missouri at the time, and it became a theme in these writings. His father was an attorney and judge, who died of pneumonia in 1847, when Twain was 11. The next year, Twain left school after the fifth grade to become a printer's apprentice. In 1851, he began working as a typesetter, contributing articles and humorous sketches to the Hannibal Journal, a newspaper that Orion owned. When he was 18, he left Hannibal and worked as a printer in New York City, Philadelphia, St. Louis, and Cincinnati, joining the newly formed International Typographical Union, the printers trade union. He educated himself in public libraries in the evenings, finding wider information than at a conventional school.

Twain describes his boyhood in Life on the Mississippi, stating that "there was but one permanent ambition" among his comrades: to be a steamboatman.

Pilot was the grandest position of all. The pilot, even in those days of trivial wages, had a princely salary – from a hundred and fifty to two hundred and fifty dollars a month, and no board to pay.

As Twain describes it, the pilot's prestige exceeded that of the captain. The pilot had to:

>...get up a warm personal acquaintanceship with every old snag and one-limbed cottonwood and every obscure wood pile that ornaments the banks of this river for twelve hundred miles; and more than that, must... actually know where these things are in the dark

Steamboat pilot Horace E. Bixby took Twain on as a cub pilot to teach him the river between New Orleans and St. Louis for $500 (equivalent to $14,000 in 2018), payable out of Twain's first wages after graduating. Twain studied the Mississippi, learning its landmarks, how to navigate its currents effectively, and how to read the river and its constantly shifting channels, reefs, submerged snags, and rocks that would "tear the life out of the strongest vessel that ever floated". It was more than two years before he received his pilot's license. Piloting also gave him his pen name from "mark twain", the leadsman's cry for a measured river depth of two fathoms (12 feet), which was safe water for a steamboat.

As a young pilot, Clemens served on the steamer A. B. Chambers with Grant Marsh, who became famous for his exploits as a steamboat captain on the Missouri River. The two liked each other, and admired one another, and maintained a correspondence for many years after Clemens left the river.

While training, Samuel convinced his younger brother Henry to work with him, and even arranged a post of mud clerk for him on the steamboat Pennsylvania. On June 13, 1858, the steamboat's boiler exploded; Henry succumbed to his wounds on June 21. Twain claimed to have foreseen this death in a dream a month earlier, which inspired his interest in parapsychology; he was an early member of the Society for Psychical Research. Twain was guilt-stricken and held himself responsible for the rest of his life. He continued to work on the river and was a river pilot until the Civil War broke out in 1861, when traffic was curtailed along the Mississippi River. At the start of hostilities, he enlisted briefly in a local Confederate unit. He later wrote the sketch "The Private History of a Campaign That Failed", describing how he and his friends had been Confederate volunteers for two weeks before disbanding.

He then left for Nevada to work for his brother Orion, who was Secretary of the Nevada Territory. Twain describes the episode in his book Roughing It.

Travels

Orion became secretary to Nevada Territory governor James W. Nye in 1861, and Twain joined him when he moved west. The brothers traveled more than two weeks on a stagecoach across the Great Plains and the Rocky Mountains, visiting the Mormon community in Salt Lake City.

Twain's journey ended in the silver-mining town of Virginia City, Nevada, where he became a miner on the Comstock Lode. He failed as a miner and went to work at the Virginia City newspaper Territorial Enterprise, working under a friend, the writer Dan DeQuille. He first used his pen name here on February 3, 1863, when he wrote a humorous travel account entitled "Letter From Carson – re: Joe Goodman; party at Gov. Johnson's; music" and signed it "Mark Twain".

His experiences in the American West inspired Roughing It, written during 1870–71 and published in 1872. His experiences in Angels Camp (in Calaveras County, California) provided material for "The Celebrated Jumping Frog of Calaveras County" (1865).

Twain moved to San Francisco in 1864, still as a journalist, and met writers such as Bret Harte and Artemus Ward. He may have been romantically involved with the poet Ina Coolbrith.

His first success as a writer came when his humorous tall tale "The Celebrated Jumping Frog of Calaveras County" was published on November 18, 1865, in the New York weekly The Saturday Press, bringing him national attention. A year later, he traveled to the Sandwich Islands (present-day Hawaii) as a reporter for the Sacramento Union. His letters to the Union were popular and became the basis for his first lectures.

In 1867, a local newspaper funded his trip to the Mediterranean aboard the Quaker City, including a tour of Europe and the Middle East. He wrote a collection of travel letters which were later compiled as The Innocents Abroad (1869). It was on this trip that he met fellow passenger Charles Langdon, who showed him a picture of his sister Olivia. Twain later claimed to have fallen in love at first sight.

Upon returning to the United States, Twain was offered honorary membership in Yale University's secret society Scroll and Key in 1868. Its devotion to "fellowship, moral and literary self-improvement, and charity" suited him well.

Marriage and children

Twain and Olivia Langdon corresponded throughout 1868. She rejected his first marriage proposal, but they were married in Elmira, New York in February 1870, where he courted her and managed to overcome her father's initial reluctance. She came from a "wealthy but liberal family"; through her, he met abolitionists, "socialists, principled atheists and activists for women's rights and social equality", including Harriet Beecher Stowe (his next-door neighbor in Hartford, Connecticut), Frederick Douglass, and writer and utopian socialist William Dean Howells, who became a long-time friend. The couple lived in Buffalo, New York, from 1869 to 1871. He owned a stake in the Buffalo Express newspaper and worked as an editor and writer. While they were living in Buffalo, their son Langdon died of diphtheria at the age of 19 months. They had three daughters: Susy (1872–1896), Clara (1874–1962), and Jean (1880–1909).

Twain moved his family to Hartford, Connecticut, where he arranged the building of a home starting in 1873. In the 1870s and 1880s, the family summered at Quarry Farm in Elmira, the home of Olivia's sister, Susan Crane. In 1874, Susan had a study built apart from the main house so that Twain would have a quiet place in which to write. Also, he smoked cigars constantly, and Susan did not want him to do so in her house.

Twain wrote many of his classic novels during his 17 years in Hartford (1874–1891) and over 20 summers at Quarry Farm. They include The Adventures of Tom Sawyer (1876), The Prince and the Pauper (1881), Life on the Mississippi (1883), Adventures of Huckleberry Finn (1884), and A

Connecticut Yankee in King Arthur's Court (1889).

The couple's marriage lasted 34 years until Olivia's death in 1904. All of the Clemens family are buried in Elmira's Woodlawn Cemetery.

Love of science and technology

Twain was fascinated with science and scientific inquiry. He developed a close and lasting friendship with Nikola Tesla, and the two spent much time together in Tesla's laboratory.

Twain patented three inventions, including an "Improvement in Adjustable and Detachable Straps for Garments" (to replace suspenders) and a history trivia game. Most commercially successful was a self-pasting scrapbook; a dried adhesive on the pages needed only to be moistened before use. Over 25,000 were sold.

Twain was an early proponent of fingerprinting as a forensic technique, featuring it in a tall tale in Life on the Mississippi (1883) and as a central plot element in the novel Pudd'nhead Wilson (1894).

Twain's novel A Connecticut Yankee in King Arthur's Court (1889) features a time traveler from the contemporary U.S., using his knowledge of science to introduce modern technology to Arthurian England. This type of historical manipulation became a trope of speculative fiction as alternate histories.

In 1909, Thomas Edison visited Twain at his home in Redding, Connecticut and filmed him. Part of the footage was used in The Prince and the Pauper (1909), a two-reel short film. It is the only known existing film footage of Twain.

Financial troubles

Twain made a substantial amount of money through his writing, but he lost a great deal through investments. He invested mostly in new inventions and technology, particularly the Paige typesetting machine. It was a beautifully engineered mechanical marvel that amazed viewers when it worked, but it was prone to breakdowns. Twain spent $300,000 (equal to $9,000,000 in inflation-adjusted terms) on it between 1880 and 1894, but before it could be perfected it was rendered obsolete by the Linotype. He lost the bulk of his book profits, as well as a substantial portion of his wife's inheritance.

Twain also lost money through his publishing house, Charles L. Webster and Company, which enjoyed initial success selling the memoirs of Ulysses S. Grant but failed soon afterward, losing money on a biography of Pope Leo XIII. Fewer than 200 copies were sold.

Twain and his family closed down their expensive Hartford home in response to the dwindling income and moved to Europe in June 1891. William M. Laffan of The New York Sun and the McClure Newspaper Syndicate offered him the publication of a series of six European letters. Twain, Olivia, and their daughter Susy were all faced with health problems, and they believed that it would be of benefit to visit European baths. The family stayed mainly in France, Germany, and Italy until May 1895, with longer spells at Berlin (winter 1891/92), Florence (fall and winter 1892/93), and Paris (winters and springs 1893/94 and 1894/95). During that period, Twain returned four times to New York due to his enduring business troubles. He took "a cheap room" in September 1893 at $1.50 per day (equivalent to $42 in 2018) at The Players Club, which he had to keep until March 1894; meanwhile, he became "the Belle of New York," in the words of biographer Albert Bigelow Paine.

Twain's writings and lectures enabled him to recover financially, combined with the help of his friend, Henry Huttleston Rogers. He began a friendship with the financier in 1893, a principal of Standard Oil, that lasted the remainder of his life. Rogers first made him file for bankruptcy in April 1894, then had him transfer the copyrights on his written works to his wife to prevent creditors from gaining possession of them. Finally, Rogers took absolute charge of Twain's money until all his creditors were paid.

Twain accepted an offer from Robert Sparrow Smythe and embarked on a year-long, around the world lecture tour in July 1895 to pay off his creditors in full, although he was no longer under any legal obligation to do so. It was a long, arduous journey and he was sick much of the time, mostly from a cold and a carbuncle. The first part of the itinerary took him across northern America to British Columbia, Canada, until the second half of August. For the second part, he sailed across the Pacific Ocean. His scheduled lecture in Honolulu, Hawaii had to be canceled due to a cholera epidemic. Twain went on to Fiji, Australia, New Zealand, Sri Lanka, India, Mauritius, and South Africa. His three months in India became the centerpiece of his 712-page book Following the Equator. In the second half of July 1896, he sailed back to England, completing his circumnavigation of the world begun 14 months before.

Twain and his family spent four more years in Europe, mainly in England and Austria (October 1897 to May 1899), with longer spells in London and Vienna. Clara had wished to study the piano under Theodor Leschetizky in Vienna. However, Jean's health did not benefit from consulting with specialists in Vienna, the "City of Doctors". The family moved to London in spring 1899, following a lead by Poultney Bigelow who had a good experience being treated by Dr. Jonas Henrik Kellgren, a Swedish osteopathic practitioner in Belgravia. They were persuaded to spend the summer at Kellgren's sanatorium by the lake in the Swedish village of Sanna. Coming back in fall, they continued the treatment in London, until Twain was convinced by lengthy inquiries in America that similar osteopathic expertise was available there.

In mid-1900, he was the guest of newspaper proprietor Hugh Gilzean-Reid at Dollis Hill House, located on the north side of London. Twain wrote that he had "never seen any place that was so satisfactorily situated, with its noble trees and stretch of country, and everything that went to make life delightful, and all within a biscuit's throw of the metropolis of the world." He then returned to America in October 1900, having earned enough to pay off his debts. In winter 1900/01, he became his country's most prominent opponent of imperialism, raising the issue in his speeches, interviews, and writings. In January 1901, he began serving as vice-president of the Anti-Imperialist League of New York.

Speaking engagements

Twain was in great demand as a featured speaker, performing solo humorous talks similar to modern stand-up comedy. He gave paid talks to many men's clubs, including the Authors' Club, Beefsteak Club, Vagabonds, White Friars, and Monday Evening Club of Hartford.

In the late 1890s, he spoke to the Savage Club in London and was elected an honorary member. He was told that only three men had been so honored, including the Prince of Wales, and he replied: "Well, it must make the Prince feel mighty fine." He visited Melbourne and Sydney in 1895 as part of a world lecture tour. In 1897, he spoke to the Concordia Press Club in Vienna as a special guest, following the diplomat Charlemagne Tower, Jr. He delivered the speech "Die Schrecken der Deutschen Sprache" ("The Horrors of the German Language")—in German—to the great amusement of the audience. In 1901, he was invited to speak at Princeton University's Cliosophic Literary Society, where he was made an honorary member.

Canadian visits

In 1881, Twain was honored at a banquet in Montreal, Canada where he made reference to securing a copyright. In 1883, he paid a brief visit to Ottawa, and he visited Toronto twice in 1884 and 1885 on a reading tour with George Washington Cable, known as the "Twins of Genius" tour.

The reason for the Toronto visits was to secure Canadian and British copyrights for his upcoming book Adventures of Huckleberry Finn, to which he had alluded in his Montreal visit. The reason for the Ottawa visit had been to secure Canadian and British copyrights for Life on the Mississippi. Publishers in Toronto had printed unauthorized editions of his books at the time, before an international copyright agreement was established in 1891. These were sold in the United States as well as in Canada, depriving him of royalties. He estimated that Belford Brothers' edition of The Adventures of Tom Sawyer alone had cost him ten thousand dollars (equivalent to $280,000 in 2018). He had unsuccessfully attempted to secure the rights for The Prince and the Pauper in 1881, in conjunction with his Montreal trip. Eventually, he received legal advice to register a copyright in Canada (for both Canada and Britain) prior to publishing in the United States, which would restrain the Canadian publishers from printing a version when the American edition was published. There was a requirement that a copyright be registered to a Canadian resident; he addressed this by his short visits to the country.

Later life and death

... the report is greatly exaggerated.

—Twain's reaction to a report of his death

Twain lived in his later years at 14 West 10th Street in Manhattan. He passed through a period of deep depression which began in 1896 when his daughter Susy died of meningitis. Olivia's death in 1904 and Jean's on December 24, 1909, deepened his gloom. On May 20, 1909, his close friend Henry Rogers died suddenly. In 1906, Twain began his autobiography in the North American Review. In April, he heard that his friend Ina Coolbrith had lost nearly all that she owned in the 1906 San Francisco earthquake, and he volunteered a few autographed portrait photographs to be sold for her benefit. To further aid Coolbrith, George Wharton James visited Twain in New York and arranged for a new portrait session. He was resistant initially, but he eventually admitted that four of the resulting images were the finest ones ever taken of him.

Twain formed a club in 1906 for girls whom he viewed as surrogate granddaughters called the Angel Fish and Aquarium Club. The dozen or so members ranged in age from 10 to 16. He exchanged letters with his "Angel Fish" girls and invited them to concerts and the theatre and to play games. Twain wrote in 1908 that the club was his "life's chief delight". In 1907, he met Dorothy Quick (aged 11) on a transatlantic crossing, beginning "a friendship that was to last until the very day of his death".

Oxford University awarded Twain an honorary doctorate in letters in 1907.

Twain was born two weeks after Halley's Comet's closest approach in 1835; he said in 1909:

I came in with Halley's Comet in 1835. It is coming again next year, and I expect to go out with it. It will be the greatest disappointment of my life if

I don't go out with Halley's Comet. The Almighty has said, no doubt: "Now here are these two unaccountable freaks; they came in together, they must go out together".

Twain's prediction was accurate; he died of a heart attack on April 21, 1910, in Redding, Connecticut, one day after the comet's closest approach to Earth.

Upon hearing of Twain's death, President William Howard Taft said:

Mark Twain gave pleasure – real intellectual enjoyment – to millions, and his works will continue to give such pleasure to millions yet to come … His humor was American, but he was nearly as much appreciated by Englishmen and people of other countries as by his own countrymen. He has made an enduring part of American literature.

Twain's funeral was at the Brick Presbyterian Church on Fifth Avenue, New York. He is buried in his wife's family plot at Woodlawn Cemetery in Elmira, New York. The Langdon family plot is marked by a 12-foot monument (two fathoms, or "mark twain") placed there by his surviving daughter Clara. There is also a smaller headstone. He expressed a preference for cremation (for example, in Life on the Mississippi), but he acknowledged that his surviving family would have the last word.

Officials in Connecticut and New York estimated the value of Twain's estate at $471,000 ($13,000,000 today).

Writing

Overview

Twain began his career writing light, humorous verse, but he became a chronicler of the vanities, hypocrisies, and murderous acts of mankind. At mid-career, he combined rich humor, sturdy narrative, and social criticism in Huckleberry Finn. He was a master of rendering colloquial speech and helped to create and popularize a distinctive American literature built on American themes and language.

Many of his works have been suppressed at times for various reasons. The

Adventures of Huckleberry Finn has been repeatedly restricted in American high schools, not least for its frequent use of the word "nigger", which was in common usage in the pre-Civil War period in which the novel was set.

A complete bibliography of Twain's works is nearly impossible to compile because of the vast number of pieces he wrote (often in obscure newspapers) and his use of several different pen names. Additionally, a large portion of his speeches and lectures have been lost or were not recorded; thus, the compilation of Twain's works is an ongoing process. Researchers rediscovered published material as recently as 1995 and 2015.

Early journalism and travelogues

Twain was writing for the Virginia City newspaper the Territorial Enterprise in 1863 when he met lawyer Tom Fitch, editor of the competing newspaper Virginia Daily Union and known as the "silver-tongued orator of the Pacific". He credited Fitch with giving him his "first really profitable lesson" in writing. "When I first began to lecture, and in my earlier writings," Twain later commented, "my sole idea was to make comic capital out of everything I saw and heard." In 1866, he presented his lecture on the Sandwich Islands to a crowd in Washoe City, Nevada. Afterwards, Fitch told him:

Clemens, your lecture was magnificent. It was eloquent, moving, sincere. Never in my entire life have I listened to such a magnificent piece of descriptive narration. But you committed one unpardonable sin – the unpardonable sin. It is a sin you must never commit again. You closed a most eloquent description, by which you had keyed your audience up to a pitch of the intensest interest, with a piece of atrocious anti-climax which nullified all the really fine effect you had produced.

It was in these days that Twain became a writer of the Sagebrush School; he was known later as its most famous member. His first important work was "The Celebrated Jumping Frog of Calaveras County," published in the New York Saturday Press on November 18, 1865. After a burst of popularity, the Sacramento Union commissioned him to write letters about his travel experiences. The first journey that he took for this job was to ride the steamer Ajax on its maiden voyage to the Sandwich Islands (Hawaii).

All the while, he was writing letters to the newspaper that were meant for publishing, chronicling his experiences with humor. These letters proved to be the genesis to his work with the San Francisco Alta California newspaper, which designated him a traveling correspondent for a trip from San Francisco to New York City via the Panama isthmus.

On June 8, 1867, he set sail on the pleasure cruiser Quaker City for five months, and this trip resulted in The Innocents Abroad or The New Pilgrims' Progress. In 1872, he published his second piece of travel literature, Roughing It, as an account of his journey from Missouri to Nevada, his subsequent life in the American West, and his visit to Hawaii. The book lampoons American and Western society in the same way that Innocents critiqued the various countries of Europe and the Middle East. His next work was The Gilded Age: A Tale of Today, his first attempt at writing a novel. The book, written with his neighbor Charles Dudley Warner, is also his only collaboration.

Twain's next work drew on his experiences on the Mississippi River. Old Times on the Mississippi was a series of sketches published in the Atlantic Monthly in 1875 featuring his disillusionment with Romanticism. Old Times eventually became the starting point for Life on the Mississippi.

Tom Sawyer and Huckleberry Finn

Twain's next major publication was The Adventures of Tom Sawyer, which draws on his youth in Hannibal. Tom Sawyer was modeled on Twain as a child, with traces of schoolmates John Briggs and Will Bowen. The book also introduces Huckleberry Finn in a supporting role, based on Twain's boyhood friend Tom Blankenship.

The Prince and the Pauper was not as well received, despite a storyline that is common in film and literature today. The book tells the story of two boys born on the same day who are physically identical, acting as a social commentary as the prince and pauper switch places. Twain had started Adventures of Huckleberry Finn (which he consistently had problems completing) and had completed his travel book A Tramp Abroad, which describes his travels through central and southern Europe.

Twain's next major published work was the Adventures of Huckleberry Finn, which confirmed him as a noteworthy American writer. Some have called it the first Great American Novel, and the book has become required reading in many schools throughout the United States. Huckleberry Finn was an offshoot from Tom Sawyer and had a more serious tone than its predecessor. Four hundred manuscript pages were written in mid-1876, right after the publication of Tom Sawyer. The last fifth of Huckleberry Finn is subject to much controversy. Some say that Twain experienced a "failure of nerve," as critic Leo Marx puts it. Ernest Hemingway once said of Huckleberry Finn:

If you read it, you must stop where the Nigger Jim is stolen from the boys. That is the real end. The rest is just cheating.

Hemingway also wrote in the same essay:

All modern American literature comes from one book by Mark Twain called Huckleberry Finn.

Near the completion of Huckleberry Finn, Twain wrote Life on the Mississippi, which is said to have heavily influenced the novel. The travel work recounts Twain's memories and new experiences after a 22-year absence from the Mississippi River. In it, he also explains that "Mark Twain" was the call made when the boat was in safe water, indicating a depth of two fathoms (12 feet or 3.7 metres).

Later writing

Twain produced President Ulysses S. Grant's Memoirs through his fledgling publishing house, Charles L. Webster & Company, which he co-owned with Charles L. Webster, his nephew by marriage.

At this time he also wrote "The Private History of a Campaign That Failed" for The Century Magazine. This piece detailed his two-week stint in a Confederate militia during the Civil War. He next focused on A Connecticut Yankee in King Arthur's Court, written with the same historical fiction style as The Prince and the Pauper. A Connecticut Yankee showed the absurdities of political and social norms by setting them in the court of King Arthur. The book was started in December 1885, then shelved a few months later until the summer of 1887, and eventually finished in the spring of 1889.

His next large-scale work was Pudd'nhead Wilson, which he wrote rapidly, as he was desperately trying to stave off bankruptcy. From November 12 to December 14, 1893, Twain wrote 60,000 words for the novel. Critics[who?] have pointed to this rushed completion as the cause of the novel's rough organization and constant disruption of the plot. This novel also contains the tale of two boys born on the same day who switch positions in life, like The Prince and the Pauper. It was first published serially in Century Magazine and, when it was finally published in book form, Pudd'nhead Wilson appeared as the main title; however, the "subtitles" make the entire title read: The Tragedy of Pudd'nhead Wilson and the Comedy of The Extraordinary Twins.

Twain's next venture was a work of straight fiction that he called Personal Recollections of Joan of Arc and dedicated to his wife. He had long said[where?] that this was the work that he was most proud of, despite the criticism that he received for it. The book had been a dream of his since childhood, and he claimed that he had found a manuscript detailing the life of Joan of Arc when he was an adolescent. This was another piece that he was convinced would save his publishing company. His financial adviser Henry Huttleston Rogers quashed that idea and got Twain out of that business altogether, but the book was published nonetheless.[citation needed]

To pay the bills and keep his business projects afloat, Twain had begun to write articles and commentary furiously, with diminishing returns, but it was not enough. He filed for bankruptcy in 1894. During this time of dire financial straits, he published several literary reviews in newspapers to help make ends meet. He famously derided James Fenimore Cooper in his article detailing Cooper's "Literary Offenses". He became an extremely outspoken critic of other authors and other critics; he suggested that, before praising Cooper's work, Thomas Lounsbury, Brander Matthews, and Wilkie Collins "ought to have read some of it".

George Eliot, Jane Austen, and Robert Louis Stevenson also fell under Twain's attack during this time period, beginning around 1890 and continuing until his death. He outlines what he considers to be "quality writing" in several letters and essays, in addition to providing a source for the "tooth and claw" style of literary criticism. He places emphasis on concision, utility of word choice, and realism; he complains, for example, that Cooper's Deerslayer purports to be realistic but has several shortcomings. Ironically, several of his own works were later criticized for lack of continuity (Adventures of Huckleberry Finn) and organization (Pudd'nhead Wilson).

Twain's wife died in 1904 while the couple were staying at the Villa di Quarto in Florence. After some time had passed he published some works that his wife, his de facto editor and censor throughout her married life, had looked down upon. The Mysterious Stranger is perhaps the best known, depicting various visits of Satan to earth. This particular work was not published in Twain's lifetime. His manuscripts included three versions, written between 1897 and 1905: the so-called Hannibal, Eseldorf, and Print Shop versions. The resulting confusion led to extensive publication of a jumbled version, and only recently have the original versions become available as Twain wrote them.

Twain's last work was his autobiography, which he dictated and thought would be most entertaining if he went off on whims and tangents in non-chronological order. Some archivists and compilers have rearranged the biography into a more conventional form, thereby eliminating some of Twain's humor and the flow of the book. The first volume of the autobiography, over 736 pages, was published by the University of California in November 2010, 100 years after his death, as Twain wished. It soon became an unexpected best-seller, making Twain one of a very few authors publishing new best-selling volumes in the 19th, 20th, and 21st centuries.

Censorship

Twain's works have been subjected to censorship efforts. According to Stuart (2013), "Leading these banning campaigns, generally, were religious organizations or individuals in positions of influence – not so much working librarians, who had been instilled with that American "library spirit" which honored intellectual freedom (within bounds of course)". In 1905, the Brooklyn Public Library banned both The Adventures of Huckleberry Finn and The Adventures of Tom Sawyer from the children's department because of their language.

Views

Twain's views became more radical as he grew older. In a letter to friend and fellow writer William Dean Howells in 1887 he acknowledged that his views had changed and developed over his lifetime, referring to one of his favorite works:

When I finished Carlyle's French Revolution in 1871, I was a Girondin; every time I have read it since, I have read it differently – being influenced and changed, little by little, by life and environment ... and now I lay the book down once more, and recognize that I am a Sansculotte! And not a pale, characterless Sansculotte, but a Marat.

Anti-imperialist

Before 1899, Twain was an ardent imperialist. In the late 1860s and early 1870s, he spoke out strongly in favor of American interests in the Hawaiian Islands. He said the war with Spain in 1898 was "the worthiest" war ever fought. In 1899, however, he reversed course. In the New York Herald, October 16, 1900, Twain describes his transformation and political awakening, in the context of the Philippine–American War, to anti-imperialism:

I wanted the American eagle to go screaming into the Pacific ... Why not spread its wings over the Philippines, I asked myself? ... I said to myself, Here are a people who have suffered for three centuries. We can make them as free as ourselves, give them a government and country of their own, put a miniature of the American Constitution afloat in the Pacific, start a brand new republic to take its place among the free nations of the world. It seemed to me a great task to which we had addressed ourselves.

But I have thought some more, since then, and I have read carefully the treaty of Paris [which ended the Spanish–American War], and I have seen that we do not intend to free, but to subjugate the people of the Philippines. We have gone there to conquer, not to redeem.

It should, it seems to me, be our pleasure and duty to make those people free, and let them deal with their own domestic questions in their own way. And so I am an anti-imperialist. I am opposed to having the eagle put its talons on any other land.

During the Boxer rebellion, Twain said that "the Boxer is a patriot. He loves his country better than he does the countries of other people. I wish him success."

From 1901, soon after his return from Europe, until his death in 1910, Twain was vice-president of the American Anti-Imperialist League, which opposed the annexation of the Philippines by the United States and had "tens of thousands of members". He wrote many political pamphlets for the organization. The Incident in the Philippines, posthumously published in 1924, was in response to the Moro Crater Massacre, in which six hundred Moros were killed. Many of his neglected and previously uncollected writings on anti-imperialism appeared for the first time in book form in 1992.

Twain was critical of imperialism in other countries as well. In Following the Equator, Twain expresses "hatred and condemnation of imperialism of all stripes". He was highly critical of European imperialists, such as Cecil Rhodes, who greatly expanded the British Empire, and Leopold II, King of the Belgians. King Leopold's Soliloquy is a stinging political satire about his private colony, the Congo Free State. Reports of outrageous exploitation and grotesque abuses led to widespread international protest in the early 1900s, arguably the first large-scale human rights movement. In the soliloquy, the King argues that bringing Christianity to the country outweighs a little starvation. Leopold's rubber gatherers were tortured, maimed and slaughtered until the movement forced Brussels to call a halt.

During the Philippine–American War, Twain wrote a short pacifist story titled The War Prayer, which makes the point that humanism and Christianity's preaching of love are incompatible with the conduct of war. It was submitted to Harper's Bazaar for publication, but on March 22, 1905, the magazine rejected the story as "not quite suited to a woman's magazine". Eight days later, Twain wrote to his friend Daniel Carter Beard, to whom he had read the story, "I don't think the prayer will be published in my time. None but the dead are permitted to tell the truth." Because he had an exclusive contract with Harper & Brothers, Twain could not publish The War Prayer elsewhere; it remained unpublished until 1923. It was republished as campaigning material by Vietnam War protesters.

Twain acknowledged that he had originally sympathized with the more moderate Girondins of the French Revolution and then shifted his sympathies to the more radical Sansculottes, indeed identifying himself as "a Marat" and writing that the Reign of Terror paled in comparison to the older terrors that preceded it. Twain supported the revolutionaries in Russia against the reformists, arguing that the Tsar must be got rid of by violent means, because peaceful ones would not work. He summed up his views of revolutions in the following statement:

I am said to be a revolutionist in my sympathies, by birth, by breeding and by principle. I am always on the side of the revolutionists, because there never was a revolution unless there were some oppressive and intolerable conditions against which to revolute.

Civil rights

Twain was an adamant supporter of the abolition of slavery and the emancipation of slaves, even going so far as to say, "Lincoln's Proclamation … not only set the black slaves free, but set the white man free also". He argued that non-whites did not receive justice in the United States, once saying, "I have seen Chinamen abused and maltreated in all the mean, cowardly ways possible to the invention of a degraded nature … but I never saw a Chinaman righted in a court of justice for wrongs thus done to him". He paid for at least one black person to attend Yale Law School and for another black person to attend a southern university to become a minister.

Twain's sympathetic views on race were not reflected in his early writings on American Indians. Of them, Twain wrote in 1870:

His heart is a cesspool of falsehood, of treachery, and of low and devilish instincts. With him, gratitude is an unknown emotion; and when one does him a kindness, it is safest to keep the face toward him, lest the reward be an arrow in the back. To accept of a favor from him is to assume a debt which you can never repay to his satisfaction, though you bankrupt yourself trying. The scum of the earth!

As counterpoint, Twain's essay on "The Literary Offenses of Fenimore Cooper" offers a much kinder view of Indians. "No, other Indians would have noticed these things, but Cooper's Indians never notice anything. Cooper thinks they are marvelous creatures for noticing, but he was almost always in error about his Indians. There was seldom a sane one among them." In his later travelogue Following the Equator (1897), Twain observes that in colonized lands all over the world, "savages" have always been wronged by "whites" in the most merciless ways, such as "robbery, humiliation, and slow, slow murder, through poverty and the white man's whiskey"; his conclusion is that "there are many humorous things in this world; among them the white man's notion that he is less savage than the other savages". In an expression that captures his East Indian experiences, he wrote, "So far as I am able to judge nothing has been left undone, either by man or Nature, to make India the most extraordinary country that the sun visits on his rounds. Where every prospect pleases, and only man is vile."

Twain was also a staunch supporter of women's rights and an active campaigner for women's suffrage. His "Votes for Women" speech, in which he pressed for the granting of voting rights to women, is considered one of the most famous in history.

Helen Keller benefited from Twain's support as she pursued her college education and publishing despite her disabilities and financial limitations. The two were friends for roughly 16 years.

Through Twain's efforts, the Connecticut legislature voted a pension for Prudence Crandall, since 1995 Connecticut's official heroine, for her efforts towards the education of African-American young ladies in Connecticut. Twain also offered to purchase for her use her former house in Canterbury, home of the Canterbury Female Boarding School, but she declined.

Labor

Twain wrote glowingly about unions in the river boating industry in Life on the Mississippi, which was read in union halls decades later. He supported the labor movement, especially one of the most important unions, the Knights of Labor. In a speech to them, he said:

Who are the oppressors? The few: the King, the capitalist, and a handful of other overseers and superintendents. Who are the oppressed? The many: the nations of the earth; the valuable personages; the workers; they that make the bread that the soft-handed and idle eat.

Religion

Twain was a Presbyterian. He was critical of organized religion and certain elements of Christianity through his later life. He wrote, for example, "Faith is believing what you know ain't so", and "If Christ were here now there is one thing he would not be – a Christian". With anti-Catholic sentiment rampant in 19th century America, Twain noted he was "educated to enmity toward everything that is Catholic". As an adult, he engaged in religious discussions and attended services, his theology developing as he wrestled with the deaths of loved ones and with his own mortality.

Twain generally avoided publishing his most controversial opinions on religion in his lifetime, and they are known from essays and stories that were published later. In the essay Three Statements of the Eighties in the 1880s, Twain stated that he believed in an almighty God, but not in any messages, revelations, holy scriptures such as the Bible, Providence, or retribution in the afterlife. He did state that "the goodness, the justice, and the mercy of God are manifested in His works", but also that "the universe is governed by strict and immutable laws", which determine "small matters", such as who dies in a pestilence. At other times, he wrote or spoke in ways that contradicted a strict deist view, for example, plainly professing a belief in Providence. In some later writings in the 1890s, he was less optimistic about the goodness of God, observing that "if our Maker is all-powerful for good or evil, He is not in His right mind". At other times, he conjectured sardonically that perhaps God had created the world with all its tortures for some purpose of His own, but was otherwise indifferent to humanity, which was too petty and insignificant to deserve His attention anyway.

In 1901, Twain criticized the actions of the missionary Dr. William Scott Ament (1851–1909) because Ament and other missionaries had collected indemnities from Chinese subjects in the aftermath of the Boxer Uprising of 1900. Twain's response to hearing of Ament's methods was published in the North American Review in February 1901: To the Person Sitting in Darkness, and deals with examples of imperialism in China, South Africa, and with the U.S. occupation of the Philippines. A subsequent article, "To My Missionary Critics" published in The North American Review in April 1901, unapologetically continues his attack, but with the focus shifted from Ament to his missionary superiors, the American Board of Commissioners for Foreign Missions.

After his death, Twain's family suppressed some of his work that was especially irreverent toward conventional religion, including Letters from the Earth, which was not published until his daughter Clara reversed her position in 1962 in response to Soviet propaganda about the withholding. The antireligious The Mysterious Stranger was published in 1916. Little Bessie, a story ridiculing Christianity, was first published in the 1972 collection Mark Twain's Fables of Man.

He raised money to build a Presbyterian Church in Nevada in 1864.

Twain created a reverent portrayal of Joan of Arc, a subject over which he had obsessed for forty years, studied for a dozen years and spent two years writing about. In 1900 and again in 1908 he stated, "I like Joan of Arc best of all my books, it is the best".

Those who knew Twain well late in life recount that he dwelt on the subject of the afterlife, his daughter Clara saying: "Sometimes he believed death ended everything, but most of the time he felt sure of a life beyond."

Twain's frankest views on religion appeared in his final work Autobiography of Mark Twain, the publication of which started in November 2010, 100 years after his death. In it, he said:

There is one notable thing about our Christianity: bad, bloody, merciless, money-grabbing, and predatory as it is – in our country particularly and in all other Christian countries in a somewhat modified degree – it is still a hundred times better than the Christianity of the Bible, with its prodigious crime – the invention of Hell. Measured by our Christianity of to-day, bad as it is, hypocritical as it is, empty and hollow as it is, neither the Deity nor his Son is a Christian, nor qualified for that moderately high place. Ours is a terrible religion. The fleets of the world could swim in spacious comfort in the innocent blood it has spilled.

Twain was a Freemason. He belonged to Polar Star Lodge No. 79 A.F.&A.M., based in St. Louis. He was initiated an Entered Apprentice on May 22, 1861, passed to the degree of Fellow Craft on June 12, and raised to the degree of Master Mason on July 10.

Twain visited Salt Lake City for two days and met there members of The Church of Jesus Christ of Latter-day Saints. They also gave him a Book of Mormon. He later wrote in Roughing It about that book:

The book seems to be merely a prosy detail of imaginary history, with the Old Testament for a model; followed by a tedious plagiarism of the New Testament.

Vivisection

Twain was opposed to the vivisection practices of his day. His objection was not on a scientific basis but rather an ethical one. He specifically cited the pain caused to the animal as his basis of his opposition:

I am not interested to know whether Vivisection produces results that are profitable to the human race or doesn't. ... The pains which it inflicts upon unconsenting animals is the basis of my enmity towards it, and it is to me sufficient justification of the enmity without looking further.

Pen names

Twain used different pen names before deciding on "Mark Twain". He signed humorous and imaginative sketches as "Josh" until 1863. Additionally, he used the pen name "Thomas Jefferson Snodgrass" for a series of humorous letters.

He maintained that his primary pen name came from his years working on Mississippi riverboats, where two fathoms, a depth indicating water safe for the passage of boat, was a measure on the sounding line. Twain is an archaic term for "two", as in "The veil of the temple was rent in twain." The riverboatman's cry was "mark twain" or, more fully, "by the mark twain", meaning "according to the mark [on the line], [the depth is] two [fathoms]", that is, "The water is 12 feet (3.7 m) deep and it is safe to pass."

Twain said that his famous pen name was not entirely his invention. In Life on the Mississippi, he wrote:

Captain Isaiah Sellers was not of literary turn or capacity, but he used to jot down brief paragraphs of plain practical information about the river, and sign them "MARK TWAIN", and give them to the New Orleans Picayune. They related to the stage and condition of the river, and were accurate and valuable; ... At the time that the telegraph brought the news of his death, I was on the Pacific coast. I was a fresh new journalist, and needed a nom de guerre; so I confiscated the ancient mariner's discarded one, and have done my best to make it remain what it was in his hands – a sign and symbol and warrant that whatever is found in its company may be gambled on as being the petrified truth; how I have succeeded, it would not be modest in me to say.

Twain's story about his pen name has been questioned by some with the suggestion that "mark twain" refers to a running bar tab that Twain would regularly incur while drinking at John Piper's saloon in Virginia City, Nevada. Samuel Clemens himself responded to this suggestion by saying, "Mark Twain was the nom de plume of one Captain Isaiah Sellers, who used to write river news over it for the New Orleans Picayune. He died in 1869 and as he could no longer need that signature, I laid violent hands upon it without asking permission of the proprietor's remains. That is the history of the nom de plume I bear."

In his autobiography, Twain writes further of Captain Sellers' use of "Mark Twain":

I was a cub pilot on the Mississippi River then, and one day I wrote a rude and crude satire which was leveled at Captain Isaiah Sellers, the oldest steamboat pilot on the Mississippi River, and the most respected, esteemed, and revered. For many years he had occasionally written brief paragraphs concerning the river and the changes which it had undergone under his observation during fifty years, and had signed these paragraphs "Mark Twain" and published them in the St. Louis and New Orleans journals. In my satire I made rude game of his reminiscences. It was a shabby poor performance, but I didn't know it, and the pilots didn't know it. The pilots thought it was brilliant. They were jealous of Sellers, because when the gray-heads among them pleased their vanity by detailing in the hearing of the younger craftsmen marvels which they had seen in the long ago on the river, Sellers was always likely to step in at the psychological moment and snuff them out with wonders of his own which made their small marvels look pale and sick. However, I have told all about this in "Old Times on the Mississippi." The pilots handed my extravagant satire to a river reporter, and it was published in the New Orleans True Delta. That poor old Captain Sellers was deeply wounded. He had never been held up to ridicule before; he was sensitive, and he never got over the hurt which I had wantonly and stupidly inflicted upon his dignity. I was proud of my performance for a while, and considered it quite wonderful, but I have changed my opinion of it long ago. Sellers never published another paragraph nor ever used his nom de guerre again.

Legacy and depictions

Trademark white suit

While Twain is often depicted wearing a white suit, modern representations suggesting that he wore them throughout his life are unfounded. Evidence suggests that Twain began wearing white suits on the lecture circuit, after the death of his wife Olivia ("Livy") in 1904. However, there is also evidence showing him wearing a white suit before 1904. In 1882, he sent a photograph of himself in a white suit to 18-year-old Edward W. Bok, later publisher of the Ladies Home Journal, with a handwritten dated note. The white suit did eventually become his trademark, as illustrated in anecdotes about this eccentricity (such as the time he wore a white summer suit to a Congressional hearing during the winter). McMasters' The Mark Twain Encyclopedia states that Twain did not wear a white suit in his last three years, except at one banquet speech.

In his autobiography, Twain writes of his early experiments with wearing white out-of-season:

Next after fine colors, I like plain white. One of my sorrows, when the summer ends, is that I must put off my cheery and comfortable white clothes and enter for the winter into the depressing captivity of the shapeless and degrading black ones. It is mid-October now, and the weather is growing cold up here in the New Hampshire hills, but it will not succeed in freezing me out of these white garments, for here the neighbors are few, and it is only of crowds that I am afraid. (Source: Wikipedia)